MURDER IN THE O.P.M.

MURDER IN THE

O.P.M.

by

ZENITH BROWN

Writing as Leslie Ford

WILDSIDE PRESS

Published by Wildside Press LLC
wildsidepress.com | bcmystery.com

1

FOR ALL THE PEOPLE WHO THINK IT improbable, not to say improper, for a woman to be involved with—at the least—more than one murder and still be invited out to dinner, I would like to say that this time it was entirely Colonel Primrose's fault. I would also like to point out that my capacity was quasi-official—or was until the morning the headlines screamed across the whole top half of the Washington papers BODY OF OPM CHIEF FOUND IN GEORGETOWN CANAL. After that it would have been difficult to keep me out.

I've sometimes had a sneaking suspicion that Colonel Primrose's activities are not so unofficial as they pretend to be. I thought it, I suppose, largely because of his rock-ribbed, viscid-eyed alter ego, Sgt. Phineas T. Buck. In spite of the fact that Colonel Primrose's card reads "92nd Engineers, U. S. A. (Retired)," and that Sergeant Buck's would read the same if he had one, nobody could have resisted the softening influence of retirement and retired pay as effectively as Buck did without some kind of military sanctions. It's true they weren't on the active roll of the 92nd Engineers, but I haven't any doubt now that the two of them had never really, at any point, been inactive or unofficial in that curious limbo of the interlocked intelligence services, and would have known the password if a sentry had held them up anywhere.

But that's probably afterthought. The day Pearl Harbor was attacked I was sure I'd seen the last of Sergeant Buck for the duration. Not even a democratic Army could be guilty of such colossal waste. I even bought some wool and started to knit him a pair of socks, which was a mistake. In the first place, he wouldn't have sold his colonel down the river to any woman for a pair of socks—not if he'd worn them, anyway—and, in the second place, he didn't go. He stayed right on with Colonel Primrose, in his old capacity of guard, philosopher and friend, in the yellow-brick house on P Street. On that winter morning when Colonel Primrose came in to see me, he was standing at such rigid attention by the door of their car that his black overcoat took on a definite cast of olive drab. His only concession to what he once called the "amendities," as I looked out, was a wooden jerk of his hand upward to the brim of his black hat. I could see the plethoric darkening of his ironbound visage, and as I closed the door behind Colonel Primrose I saw him turn and spit over the fender into the icy gutter as accurately as Nazi artillery fire. If I ever do manage to marry the colonel, I haven't the slightest doubt he'll picket the church, and I hate to think what his sign will read.

It was the first time I'd seen either of them for several weeks. Even before Pearl Harbor, their mysterious junkets out of town had become more and more frequent, and the secrecy around them more and more impenetrable. I could always tell how successful they'd been by the way Colonel Primrose sat down in the leather wing chair in the safe haven of the garden sitting room of my Georgetown house, not far from his own on P Street. But this morning he didn't sit down at all. He went over to the fire and held his hands out to it a moment. Then he turned around.

"You've heard of Washington's so-called social lobby, haven't you, Mrs. Latham?" he asked with a smile.

"Don't tell me you're buying shoes for the Army and have just been invited to dinner with somebody who's got a lot to sell?" I answered.

I sat down on the sofa, watching him a little anxiously. He looked tired. The humor and resiliency that make him normally look less than his fifty-five years were gone. By the way he moved his head I could tell that the wound he'd got in his neck at the Argonne was bothering him again, as it did when he went without sleep too long. His hair looked grayer, and the twinkle that usually warmed his black eyes when he talked to me was gone. Whatever it was they'd been doing was still undone, and he was worried and discouraged. I'd seen him worried many times. I'd seldom seen him discouraged.

"No," he said. He smiled faintly again. "At least not that I'm aware of. I'm on the receiving end myself, this time. There's a man here that I want to meet casually and off the record. I thought I could probably get you to ask him and his wife in for dinner."

"Do I know them?"

"If you don't, you will. They've just come, and they'll be everywhere sooner or later. I'll probably run into him myself, but time is of the essence, and I haven't got much of it to spend at parties these days. If you haven't met them, do so at once and have them in."

I looked up at him with astonishment. It was the first time since I'd known him that he'd got me mixed up with Sergeant Buck. For a moment I was pretty amazed.

"That's an order, I take it," I said, acid-sweet.

He looked at me quickly. I hadn't realized it was possible for him to flush, but he did. "I'm sorry," he said abruptly. "I didn't mean it that way. I'm tired, I guess. I'm the last person in the world who'd try to order you around, my dear—or want to. You must know that. I'm asking your help in a matter of importance."

"In that case, I'll be delighted," I said. "Who is it? And what's he done? Or am I allowed to ask questions?"

He smiled at that. "I don't just know how I could stop you," he said blandly. "I can even answer that one. I don't know that he's done anything—or that he's left anything undone, which concerns me even more right now. That's what I'm trying to find out. It's

Lawrason Hilyard I'm interested in. Have you met either of them?"

"He's one of the dollar-a-year men in OPM, isn't he?" I asked.

Colonel Primrose nodded. "He's attached to OPM. Officially he's an assistant branch chief. Actually he has a sort of special liaison job between OPM, the Board of Economic Warfare and Army and Navy procurement. And I want to meet him."

"Couldn't you just get a taxi and go to his office? And save everybody a lot of trouble? After all——"

He interrupted me placidly. "Don't be naïve, Mrs. Latham. I could—very easily. I could also phone him and ask him to come to my office. That's precisely what I'm trying to avoid—as you're perfectly well aware. You haven't answered my question. Have you met them?"

"No, I haven't," I said. I got up and went over to my desk. "But I can, very simply."

I pulled a batch of papers out of the pigeonhole where I keep the letters I'm going to answer someday and the memoranda of things I'm going to do if there's ever time. It's usually so full I have to put its whole contents in the fire periodically to make room for new entries. The letter I was hunting for would probably have gone that route if it hadn't been for Colonel Primrose, merely because even now there are only twenty-four hours a day in Washington, and the friends of friends descend like locusts—or like wolves on the fold, some people say. I got the letter out and put the rest of them back.

"A friend of mine who used to live here asked me to call on them," I said. I went back to the sofa. The letter was quite thick. I saw Colonel Primrose brighten instantly. He cocked his head down, the way he does, and his eyes sharpened like an old parrot's.

"What do you think he's done, or hasn't done?" I asked.

He came over and sat down beside me. "That's blackmail, I suppose you know," he said pleasantly. Then his face went so serious suddenly that I was a little ashamed of myself.

"I don't want to know, really," I said.

"I hadn't planned to tell you. But if you have common friends, you might find out some of the things I haven't been able to find out myself. It's important— and confidential."

"Then don't tell me," I said. "I'm very bad at——"

He interrupted me. "Have you ever heard of promethium?"

"I've heard of Prometheus in Greek mythology."

"That's where the word comes from. Just as titanium comes from Titan. Promethium is a metal like titanium, iridium and beryllium. It's used chiefly as an alloy to harden softer metals like copper and aluminum. It's important already, and on the priorities list, but——"

He hesitated for a moment.

"——if certain conditions can be met, it's going to be allocated, and it will be perhaps the most important of the critical and strategic metals. If the Navy can get what it wants, the submarine battle of the Pacific is won before we really start. It's that important. I can't go into it, but at New London last week a naval officer called it the 'magic metal.' That's literally what it is."

"And how does it tie in with Lawrason Hilyard?" I asked.

"He produces virtually the entire output of promethium in this country," Colonel Primrose said quietly. "He also issues the priorities on it for OPM. In one capacity or another, he comes as near one-man control of a strategic material as is possible today."

"Dishonestly?"

"Not at all. Or there's no evidence to that effect. Practically everybody who can't get an A-1-A or at least an A-1 priority rating on anything he wants says it's because somebody in OPM is sitting on it for his own benefit. That's to be expected. From all I hear of Hilyard he's a good citizen."

"Then why——"

"Ask me later," he said. "Now, what's in that letter? Read it to me."

"It's from Agnes Philips," I said, opening it. "She used to live here."

I read it to him. " 'Grace dear,' " it said. " 'You'll be furious, but will you, for me, come out of your cave dwelling and call on the Lawrason Hilyards? He's an angel and responsible for all the cakes and ale—including the lovely new swimming pool—the Philipses are now happily enjoying. You'll adore him, and since no man ever married the woman people who like him would have picked out for him, I've said all you need to know about Mrs. H.— except that the nest egg was hers, from a previous husband.

" 'But Lawrason and Myrtle aren't the point. It's Diane. I want you to do something about her. Diane's twenty-two, almost twenty-three. She looks like a Fragonard, and she's all violet and pale gold, except, unfortunately, a little promethium dropped into the ladle when the angels were pouring her out——' "

I stopped and looked at Colonel Primrose. Apparently I had heard of promethium.

He smiled. "In a two-per-cent promethium alloy, copper cuts the toughest steel in existence, Mrs. Latham," he said blandly.

"She . . . does sound awful," I said. I went back to Agnes' letter.

" '——so that "difficult" isn't quite strong enough and her family don't like to call her any of the more modern terms. We think she's a lamb, personally, but the young man wouldn't have been our son-in-law, and I suppose that always makes a difference. Although I never met him, really. Lawrason and Myrtle broke it up before we came three years ago, and since then this place has had a stag line that reads like an American Almanach de Gotha. But the lady always says No. If you could produce a socially presentable, well-born young man—he doesn't have to have money, now—that Diane would marry, Myrtle would pay you a million dollars. You'd better think it over—you'll need money March fifteenth.' "

I stopped and looked at Colonel Primrose. "Shall I read any more?"

He nodded calmly. "If you please, Mrs. Latham."

" 'I can't tell you anything but village gossip about Bowen Digges, called "Bo," ' " I read. " 'It was his name as much as anything the family didn't like. He came from the wrong side of the tracks. Father dead, mother ran a roadside store and service station. He worked up from water boy to wash-up man in the laboratory at seventy-five dollars a month, which august job he had when he decided to marry the boss' daughter. It was one American success story that flopped. They paid him twenty-five hundred dollars to abandon the idea, which he did promptly and beat it. That piqued Diane. I'd have been pretty mad myself. It was certainly shortsighted, as Diane, her sister Joan and a son by Lawrason's first wife are the only heirs. But Bo must have heard about the bird in the hand.

" 'All that was five years ago, and should be water under the bridge. But somehow it isn't. That's one of the reasons Myrtle decided to go to Washington with Lawrason and take a house. Once I asked Diane if she was still in love with Bo. She turned those amazing hyacinth eyes on me and said, "When he wanted twenty-five hundred dollars more than he did me?" So that's that. Anyway, I wish you'd call on them and see they get around, and that Diane meets the cream of the crop. There's something about her that makes my heart hurt. I don't know what it is. Maybe you can do something about her mother, even. Does Lilac happen to make good arsenic soup?' "

I turned to the end of the letter. "That's all about the Hilyards, except a couple of postscripts.

" 'P. S.: You'll probably hear them play the other side of the record about Lawrason, with "ruthless" as the leitmotiv. There's probably something in it, but he's been wonderful to us. Diane's the only thing I've ever disagreed with him about—and only once openly.

" 'P. P. S.: If you're tired of being a widow, darling, I'd suggest Myrtle Hilyard's brother, Bartlett Folger, who'll be around there with them. So far, nobody's been smart enough to get him to the altar, and he's got a lovely place out here.'

"And that's all," I said.

"When you're tired of being a widow, Mrs. Latham," Colonel Primrose remarked, "I trust you'll remember my application for priority rating has been on your desk for some time?"

"Thank you, sir," I said. I put the letter back in the envelope. "Would you like me to call on the Hilyards this afternoon?"

He smiled. "I would, very much." He held out his hand. "May I see that letter?"

I gave it to him. He read the first part of it through slowly, frowning a little.

"Did I leave something out?"

He shook his head. "No. I was just interested." He gave the letter back to me, got up and stood for a moment looking absently at the fire. Then he said, "You don't mind asking them for dinner for me, do you? It might be a good plan to have Diane, too, if you will."

"And Mr. Bartlett Folger?" I asked.

He smiled. "I'd like to say let's skip him, but since this is business, not pleasure, I think it's a very good idea."

I went to the desk and got my calendar. It was full for almost a month.

"I can cancel the Martins' dinner Friday," I said, "if I can get the Hilyards then."

"That's fine."

He started for the door. Almost there, he turned around and smiled again.

"I think I'm going to enjoy working with you officially for once, Mrs. Latham," he said. "It will also be a pleasure not to have a body for you to stumble over, just for once."

He was partly right, because it was a stray tramp who stumbled over Lawrason Hilyard's body, not I. It was the next Wednesday morning he did it—two days before the Hilyards and Diane and her uncle, Bartlett Folger, were coming to my house to dine.

2

B Y FIVE O'CLOCK, WHEN I SET OUT TO CALL
on the Lawrason Hilyards, I had picked up a consid-
able amount of what might be called background material. Backstairs material would be a more accurate
term, I suppose, since it came mostly from Lilac, my
colored cook, while she was serving my lunch. Lilac,
a ranking blossom in the Rosebud Chapter of the
Daughters of the Nile and a member of the Vigilantes
Committee of her church, gets the local news even
ahead of the gossip writers, and from a slightly different angle. Her angle on national and international affairs is also slightly different, because the only authorities in those fields that she has the least respect for are
the laundryman and the policy man who collects her
burial insurance Monday mornings at ten o'clock. When
I have lunch or dinner alone I can hear as much of the
news and comment on both fronts as I care to hear.
Nevertheless, I was surprised when she came waddling
to the service table by the door with my soup plate.

"Did Ah hear you an' th' colonel talkin' 'bout some
people named Hilyers?" she asked.

I nodded. Lilac's been with me since before my elder
son Bill was born and through all the major crises of

my life, and I don't suppose anything goes on in the house that she doesn't know all about.

"Boston, he's workin' for them," she said. "Leas' he was," she added darkly. "Boston ain' never worked for them kind of people be-fore."

"What's the matter with them?" I asked casually.

"Ah don' say they's nothin' the matter with 'em," Lilac answered. "You know Boston. He's light. Ah don' mean part white. Ah mean jus' natchurly light . . . an' fiery."

I knew Boston. He used to be Agnes Philips' mother's butler, and I suppose the Hilyards had got him through Agnes, or she'd have asked me to help them find servants too. I hadn't realized he was particularly fiery. Nevertheless, according to Lilac, he didn't think much of the Hilyards. It seems that they paid one thousand dollars a month for the house that General Ralston's wife was delighted to get three hundred dollars for in normal times, and boggled at paying Annie and Boston one hundred and twenty-five dollars as cook and butler. Mrs. Hilyard ordered tom turkeys instead of hens, which is a crime of no mean order, in Lilac's opinion. She also insisted that the vegetables be cooked in their skins in half a cup of water to save what Lilac calls the vittlemans and doesn't believe in, and she was always poking around in the kitchen.

But there's no use arguing with Lilac. I said, "Really?" and went on with my lunch.

"When they firs' come," she went on ominously,

"butter wouldn't melt in they mouf. Now they fights like cats an' dogs."

I looked up with surprise.

"Specially since that man come," she added.

"What man?"

"Ah don' know what man. Ah jus' sayin' what Boston say las' night. The man tha's hangin' roun' over there all time, talkin' 'bout the devil. 'Bout he goin' to th' bad place when he die."

I started to put down my napkin and demand some sense out of all this, but I restrained myself, knowing it was the surest way to make her shiny ebony face go stolidly blank and send her muttering away to the kitchen.

"Do you mean Mr. Hilyard's going to hell?" I asked.

"He already there," Lilac said. "He don' call his soul his own, Boston say. It's th' man Ah'm talkin' about. Th' man hangin' roun'. Th' devil's goin' to get his own self, he keep on sayin'. Mis' Hilyer she don' let him in th' house. One day she go out an' drive him away her own self. It's excitement times over that place. Boston ain' used to workin' for them kind of people."

She hadn't mentioned Diane Hilyard. I was thinking about that, and wondering why, as I parked my car in front of the white brick mansion in Prospect Street that the Hilyards were paying a thousand dollars a month for. It's one of Georgetown's distinguished houses, built before anyone had thought of the Federal City that now overshadows Georgetown and most of the world. It occupies most of the block along 37th Street across from the campus of Georgetown University. Its gardens, which used to run down to the river, are cut off now at the stone embankment they built when they put through the Chesapeake and Ohio Canal toward the beginning of the last century. The Ralstons bought it when he was chief of staff after the last war, and did a very intelligent job of changing it from a low-class rooming house back to a lot of its former glory. I remember when it seemed miles away from everything, even in the '20's, but now that Washington's spread like a bottleful of ink on a clean blotter, it's practically on the White House steps.

I pressed the bell and waited. In a moment I heard a chain rattle lightly and slip into its metal groove. The door opened about six inches, and Boston peered out cautiously. His face broke instantly into a warm grin. He unhooked the chain and greeted me with a mixture of cordiality and relief that more than confirmed everything Lilac had said.

"Certainly glad to see you, Miss Grace. Will you res' your wraps? How you been keepin', an' how them boys?"

"We're all fine, thank you, Boston," I said. "How have you been? Is Mrs. Hilyard at home?"

I saw him glance across the street where the gray stone wall of Georgetown campus ends in a broken jagged line along 37th Street. It seemed to me that his face had the mingled anxiety and fascination that Lilac's has when she talks about a haunted house a friend of mine owns in Fairfax.

"Lilac tells me you've had a strange man around," I said, giving him my fur coat.

He looked quickly along the hall. "'Deed she ain' ought to mentioned that to nobody, Miss Grace," he whispered. "Th' madam she say she don' want people talkin' 'bout that."

"I won't breathe a word," I said.

"Ah'll 'preciate that, Miss Grace, 'deed Ah will," he said. He was so definitely relieved that I gathered there'd been some sharp instructions on the subject quite recently, and that he liked his job at least well enough not to want to lose it.

"Right this way, Miss Grace. Ah'll tell Mis' Hilyard."

He opened the door of the small drawing room on the left, and I went in. Mrs. Ralston had taken the hundreds of signed photographs of notables from the tables and mantel, otherwise the room was familiarly the same.

It sometimes seems to me that houses and furniture and servants are the only things that give Washington any basic and recognizable continuity, though I might throw in Senator Glass and Senator Norris. Everything else changes so fast—in spite of the present long tenancy in high places—that it's hard to tell from one day to another who'll be sitting on whose Louis Quinze needle-point chairs. I'd sat on those in this room under at least a dozen chatelaines, with their owner taking over from time to time in between, when she had a debutante granddaughter to introduce and later to marry. It's a room that always fascinates me, because a British officer billeted there long ago engraved the face of His Majesty George III on the pink marble panel under the mantel, just above a startled fawn being brought down, with the pack coming up in full cry. I went over to look at it again, and then I stopped.

Through the white paneled door into the large drawing room I heard a sharp and very cutting female voice:

". . . forgotten whose money you started on! It was mine! You're a coward! You're afraid of that——"

She stopped abruptly as she heard Boston's knock on the door. It must have been his second or third, I thought, unless he'd been standing there with his knees shaking. And I shouldn't have blamed him. I never heard a voice that had such cool and unadulterated malignity in it. I was so startled by it myself that I couldn't have moved if I'd wanted to. I did move in an instant, however, to a sofa by the front window as far from that door as I could get. I felt as if it would open and a she-dragon sail in and off with my head in an instant. I saw the point of the arsenic soup at once.

That's why I was totally unprepared for the woman who came in through the hall door a moment later, closing it behind her.

"Oh, Mrs. Latham, it's so nice to see you," she said.

"Agnes Philips has told us so much about you. I just feel as if I'd known you for years!"

She held out her hand cordially. Mine must have felt like a wet, very dead fish.

Myrtle Hilyard was a tall woman, with snow-white, smartly coifed hair and large liquid-soft dark eyes. Her voice was almost affectedly gentle and low-pitched, though I mightn't have thought that if I hadn't heard it high-pitched and anything but gentle the moment before. I even wondered for an instant if I had heard her—if I hadn't imagined it or it had been someone else speaking. She sat down beside me on the sofa, reached for a blue silk knitting bag lying on the porphyry-topped table and took out a half-finished dark blue sweater.

"I was just saying to my husband I hoped Agnes had written you we were here," she was saying. "He did so much want to come in and meet you, but he's late for a conference and has to rush off immediately. I don't know how he stands the pace, really. I'm seriously thinking of taking him back home."

"But you've just come," I said.

"I know, but I really think he's going to have to resign." Mrs. Hilyard clicked her ivory needles efficiently. "He isn't physically up to the demands they make on him. And frankly, my dear, he's so discouraged at the confusion and lack of direction of all of it that I'm afraid of his health. You'd think in times like these people could forget politics."

"Haven't they, in the OPM?" I asked.

"My dear, if you only knew."

She raised her brown eyes and looked at me earnestly. The difference between what she had made herself and what she was was so sharp, all of a sudden, that it startled me. If she hadn't been knitting I doubt if I'd have noticed it, but there was her face, limpid-eyed and gentle, and below it her hands, strong and determined, eating off the yarn with swift, almost machine-like precision, the staccato click of the needles completely belying the concerned affection in her voice.

"I do hope you'll dine with me before you leave," I said. "I want to hear about Agnes and Tom. Could you come this Friday, do you think?"

"We'd love to. It's so sweet of you," she said promptly. "Everyone's so busy. I was saying to my husband I've never seen people so really busy. Of course I don't want you to say anything about my husband resigning. Somebody could make political capital out of it, and it's just his health, really."

She moved a little in her seat. A big black limousine had drawn up in front of the curb, and a man who certainly didn't look as if his health was in even the remotest jeopardy crossed the sidewalk to the open door.

"There he goes now," Mrs. Hilyard said pleasantly.

Lawrason Hilyard was above middle height, with ruddy cheeks and an air of abounding vitality that was apparent in every line and movement of his well-set-up body. He stopped beside the stone mounting block with the little ice-covered puddle on it where generations of feet had worn it down, and glanced quickly across the street. I felt Mrs. Hilyard's body tense. She leaned across the back of the sofa and tapped on the window. Lawrason Hilyard turned. The expression on his face was not particularly cordial, I may say, nor did the smile on her face as she waved good-by to him seem entirely genuine.

Then I realized she was not waving good-by to him. She was motioning to him to get in the car and go on. And the reason was obvious. A man was crossing the street from the corner by the wall, his hand up. I had the impression that Mr. Hilyard had intended to stop and speak to him until he heard the tap on the window. He got into the car at once, and by the time the man was across the road there was nothing but an empty space where the big limousine had been.

The man stood there, his hat in his hand, looking after it blankly. There wasn't anything dreadfully terrifying about him that I could see. He was tall and thin, with thin straggly gray hair, and if anybody's health was in danger, it would be his, I thought. His overcoat was threadbare and shoddy, and his hand was blue with cold as he raised it to put his hat back on. The hat was new, and his shoes were polished neatly, although they were old and out of shape. I had an impression of something rather sweet and other-worldly in his face in the fleeting glimpse of it that I got as he looked up at the window, before he turned and went slowly across the street again.

Mrs. Hilyard turned back and went on with her knitting, accelerating the pace considerably.

"Are there many beggars around Washington?" she asked casually.

"Not that I've seen," I said. "Why?"

"I just wondered."

The implication being sufficiently made, she changed the subject.

"Of course, I was very much surprised when I got here. Agnes engaged this house for us. It's very nice, of course, and I understand it's considered smart to live in Georgetown. It seems awfully run-down and dilapidated to me. My daughter Joan laughs at me. She lives up the street. Her husband's with the Board of Economic Warfare. I said to my husband it's lovely to have all the family together again. My brother is here, too, you know. He's living on his yacht, down by that awful fish market."

"Won't you bring him to dinner too?" I asked. "And your younger daughter? Agnes said she's lovely."

"If she isn't going out, I'm sure she'd enjoy it very much," Mrs. Hilyard said. She looked up from her knitting. "I wonder if by any chance you've ever heard of a young man named Stanley Woland?"

If she'd asked me if I'd ever heard of the Washington Monument I should have been less surprised. Stanley Woland, whose name until recently had been Count Stanislaus Wolanski, was not what I should have called a young man, exactly. Until the war had brought a lot of personable unattached men to Washington he was the extra man whom everyone could always count on. Even after the legation he served as fourth or fifth secretary ceased functioning as an independent organization, he was still around with his moldy title, being charming to older women. For a moment I started to say, "I do hope Diane isn't seeing very much of Mr. Stanley Woland." Fortunately, I didn't, for just then a maroon sports car aglitter with an extraordinary amount of the metals that are now critically important for war drew up in front of the house, its top down to the winter winds. A man in a fur-lined overcoat, a jaunty gray hat with a parrot's feather in the band, and yellow chamois gloves, leaped out, slammed the door and bounded across the sidewalk and up the steps.

Mrs. Hilyard put her knitting back into the *moiré* bag and zipped it up with a pleased, even excited, air.

I got up. "I must be going," I said.

"Oh, no, my dear. I do want you to meet Stanley. He's such a pet. And you haven't met Diane. You know, we met Stanley entirely by accident. He was motoring through our town and his car broke down right in front of our place."

"Really?" I said. "It doesn't surprise me in the least."

"What's that?" she asked quickly.

I didn't have to answer. Stanley was in the room. Some people say he bounds about like a gazelle to prove his knees aren't stiff yet, but I think that's unfair. I think he was told it was gay and attractive and believed it.

"You dear boy!" Mrs. Hilyard cried, and Stanley, with that fine old old-world courtesy that women still seem to love, clicked his heels and kissed her hand. The bald spot on the top of his head always shows when he does, but probably he doesn't know it yet. "This is Mrs. Latham, a friend of——"

"Hello, Stanley," I said.

"Hello, Grace."

Stanley looked as if he'd like to throttle me on the spot. I gathered he didn't feel well enough entrenched in the Hilyard household to have too many of his old friends about.

"Isn't it nice that our two friends in Washington know each other?" Mrs. Hilyard said delightedly. And just then something happened to her face. I looked quickly around at the door, and if, as I thought, even Stanley Woland caught his breath, I wasn't surprised.

By all odds the loveliest girl I've seen in Washington in a good many seasons was standing there. She had the most extraordinary coloring. Her hair was pale sunlit gold, and her eyes were as violet as an evening sky. She had on a periwinkle skirt and sweater, and she looked much nearer seventeen than twenty-two, going on twenty-three. Except for an almost imperceptible something around her full red mouth that I couldn't name, her face was as expressionless as a pool of water, or as the faces in repose of most of her contemporaries. It wasn't blank exactly, or sullen, and not bored, but rather just exceptionally unimpressed with the need of being anything she didn't feel like

being. You would certainly never get the idea, looking at her, that she'd ever shed a tear, or that anything had ever affected her very deeply.

"Diane!" Stanley sprang forward and held out his
hand. He didn't kiss hers—he had far too much social
sense for that—but the admiration in his manner was
more than apparent, and very genuine.

She smiled at him. For an instant her whole face
lighted up. My heart gave a funny little downward
bump. Her mother was beaming with that sort of fatu-
ous pleasure that parents show when recalcitrant children unexpectedly toe the line. I'd felt it on my own
face when my sons were dancing with my friends'
younger daughters after they'd said, "Oh, mother,
what a lump!"

Diane Hilyard came across the rug with her hand
out. "You're Grace Latham, aren't you? Agnes told me
about you. I thought you'd look older."

Her eyes were level with mine and very clear and
steady, as if she was measuring me against some stand-
ard she had all her own.

"Grace has been a charming young widow for years
and years," Stanley remarked, without rancor. "Ever
since I first came to Washington, in fact."

We smiled at each other. It seemed to me best just
then not to make any of the obvious retorts.

Diane Hilyard still had hold of my hand. I don't
know why I had the feeling that she wanted to ask me
something, but I did.

"I'm glad you came to see us," she said.

"I'll see you again soon, I hope." I smiled at her and looked at Stanley. I wasn't going to see very much of her at all, I knew, if he could help it. People who eat their cake and have it too are always afraid somebody's going to tell on them, especially when they've decided to stake out a permanent claim on the shifting sands of life. However, I doubt if at that point Stanley needed to be worried about me. If he wanted to marry Diane Hilyard and she was willing to marry him, it wasn't any business of mine. I even liked him, in a way.

I switched on my motor and started along Prospect Street. It had begun to snow a little, the flakes falling softly across the headlights. I slowed down as I got to the stop sign at 33rd Street, and glanced at the man standing there on the curb. It was Mrs. Hilyard's "beggar." For an instant I had an impulse to lean over, lower the window and ask him if I couldn't take him somewhere. I should have done it, I think, if it hadn't been dark, and I wish now I had. I've obeyed much foolisher impulses in my time. But just then the capital streets weren't awfully safe for women anyway, and it seemed wiser not to. He stood there for a moment when he could have crossed, and as I pressed my foot on the gas I saw him turn slowly and go back the way he'd come. For the first time I was a little uneasy about him. There was something purposeful about the way he was refusing to give up.

3

ONCE YOU BECOME CONSCIOUS OF A word it starts dogging you everywhere you go. That happened to me with promethium. Until Colonel Primrose mentioned it that Monday morning, I'd hardly been aware of having heard it before. By midnight I decided I must have been deaf ever to have missed it. And the same thing is true of people. If anyone I knew had been seeing any of the Hilyards, they hadn't mentioned it to me—not, at least, so that it had made an impression on my mind. Now, all of a sudden, Hilyards in one form or another began popping up all over the place.

I stopped in, on my way home from Prospect Street, to a cocktail party some friends on 29th Street were having. I drew up at the curb behind another car that was just arriving, and opened my door. As I did I saw the hands of the clock on the dash standing at ten minutes to six. I reached back and switched on the radio to listen to the news a moment before I went in. Before I could turn it lower, the voice of a well-known commentator was blaring out into the night:

" '. . . is promethium, one of the most critical, if not the most——' "

I turned it down quickly.

" '——of the minor metals needed in the war program today,' the congressman said on the floor of the House of Representatives this afternoon. 'Why then,' he demanded, 'has no price ceiling been put on this precious metal? Why have no steps been taken to requisition the entire output of this life sinew of war for war use only? Will I-Day—and by I-Day I mean Investigation Day, the Day of Reckoning—show a bleeding nation that somebody has feathered his own nest at the expense of democracy in travail?' "

I turned my head. The man and girl from the car just ahead of me had stopped halfway across the sidewalk. They were standing there perfectly rigid, as if that first blast of sound had frozen them in their tracks. The girl's face was turned toward me. It was as white as the snowflakes settling down on the shoulders of her long mink coat, and the band of mink around her hat. As the commentator switched to news from the European front the man gave her arm a tug. She turned and followed him mechanically across the sidewalk and up the steps. After a moment I turned off the radio and went along after them.

The rooms were crowded, but not so densely that you couldn't distinguish between familiar and unfamiliar faces. Most of these were unfamiliar, and I heard another old cave dweller with a jet-bead band to hold up her sagging chin say stridently to our hostess, "My dear, where did you find all these attractive people? It's such a relief from the early New Deal days! They're almost as attractive as the group in the last war!"

My host took me by the arm. "There's an interesting chap over here I want you to talk to," he said, piloting me toward a corner by the piano.

"Won't anybody else talk to him?" I demanded.

I was trying to spot the man and girl who came in just ahead of me, but they were lost in the crowd. I was also trying to say hello to people I knew as I was being propelled along.

"Hello, Grace," somebody said. "Where's the colonel?"

I turned to see which familiar face that came from, and answer it. As a result, all I heard above the sound and fury was the young man by the piano saying, "How do you do, Mrs. Latham." Then my host, having thrust a Martini into my hand, was gone, and the interesting young man was waiting for me to say something. So I said, "Have you been in Washington long?"—which is always safe, if not exciting.

"Three months," he said. "I'm at OPM."

I said, "Really?" and just then I saw the girl with the mink hat and white face. She was looking over our way. As our eyes met she turned her head quickly, two bright pink spots in her cheeks, and I saw her speak to the man beside her. I could almost hear her "Don't look now, but over there by the piano——" He seemed to freeze again, the way they both had on the sidewalk, and after a second turned with pretty elaborate casualness and looked toward our corner.

I looked up at the young man beside me. He was quite tall and had a pleasant, self-possessed and detached kind of air. It wouldn't have made the least difference to him if nobody had talked to him at all. He'd apparently been quietly enjoying himself from the side line.

"You don't happen to know those two people, do you?" I asked.

"Which two people?"

"The girl with the yellow wool dress with the topaz necklace and mink hat. And the large young man in the brown striped suit with her."

"With the clean collar and his hair combed?"

I glanced up at him. He grinned and ran his hand over the rather tousled mess on the top of his own head. It wasn't *not* combed, it was just that kind of hair. But I saw what he meant. The other young man was almost painfully neat.

"That's them," I answered.

He shook his head. "Nope. I don't know them," he said amiably. "I know their names, if that's any good to you. It's socially I don't know them." He seemed to be having a very good time, someway. There was an infectious twinkle in his gray eyes that was even a little exasperating.

"What's the matter with them?" I asked.

"Not a thing. They're impeccable, absolutely. His name is Carey Eaton. He's with the Board of Economic Warfare. Her name is Mrs. Carey Eaton. Her father's my boss at OPM. His name is Lawrason Hilyard."

"Oh," I said. "I see."

"What do you see?"

"Why the radio announcement about promethium got her so upset."

He looked at me oddly. "What about promethium?"

"A congressman said not enough had been done about it," I said. "About price control and requisitioning of supplies, and was somebody putting self-interest above defense. You know."

"That's interesting," he said slowly. "I've been wondering——"

He stopped for an instant.

"As a matter of fact, Hilyard's an honest guy. People that say he keeps certain firms from getting supplies are crazy. I sit right under him and check on every application that comes in." He swallowed a shrimp covered with mayonnaise and grinned. "I hate to have to say this, Mrs. Latham, because I hate his guts."

I looked at him in astonishment. "Will you please tell me who you are?" I demanded. "And where you come from? And what you're doing here?"

"I'm supposed to be an engineer," he said good-humoredly. "I come from California. Used to teach metallurgical chemistry, if you know what that is. If you mean what am I doing at this party, I couldn't tell you, except that our esteemed host is a lawyer, and he has a guest whose name is Duncan Scott. Duncan Scott is also a lawyer, and he's been hanging around OPM for a week trying to pry loose a couple of hundred pounds of promethium for a client in Ohio. He can't see Mr. Hilyard, so he decided to see me. And I can't do anything for him, if it interests you. There just isn't any promethium."

"I see," I said.

He looked at me skeptically. "You don't happen to be a small businessman, do you, Mrs. Latham?"

"No," I said. "Why?"

"Because the reason I'm backed up against the corner behind the piano is to get away from one," he said. "He doesn't believe there isn't any promethium either. He's retained our host to put on the screws." His face sobered. "I sound like a bureaucratic goon, don't I? I'm not, as a matter of fact. I feel sorry for those poor guys cooling their heels down here, trying to get stuff to keep their plants going. I don't blame them for being fighting mad, if they'd be mad at the right people. Now take my friend Mr. Ira Colton over there."

He nodded at a short square man in a gray suit and red tie, talking much too loudly to a bored young man from the Division of Far Eastern Affairs of the State Department whom he'd cornered near the fireplace.

"He's got a specialty plant in a small town near Cleveland. He figured out a way to make a one-per-cent alloy of promethium and low-grade aluminum, and he makes bright shiny gadgets they put cosmetics in. He hires about fifty people, and he's absolutely washed up. He's got hold of some aluminum—bootleg, is my guess—but he can't get his promethium. He's spending what money he's got left retaining a lawyer. The lawyer will tell him in a month or so what he got straight from the horse's mouth two weeks ago—that there just is not any promethium for lipstick containers, or for much else, as a matter of fact."

"There really isn't?" I said.

"There really isn't. I know some people are saying Lawrason Hilyard has a lot piled up in his attic, or someplace. That's baloney. We know the output and we can account for every molecule of it. If Hilyard had a nerve in his body and his hide wasn't armor plate, he'd get a hole and crawl in it."

"You don't think he's apt to resign?"

The young man from California looked down at me and shook his head.

"Resign? Lady, when Lawrason Hilyard resigns, it's going to be because the undertaker's waiting in the next room. He loves it. He's where his wife can't get him on the telephone, for once in his life. We've got two big signs in our room. One says Time is Short, and the other says, Tell Mrs. Hilyard the Boss is Out."

"Have they ever asked you there for tea?" I inquired.

"Nope," he said.

"There's another daughter. She's beautiful. Much prettier than"—I looked around for Mrs. Eaton, but she and her husband were gone—"than this one."

"So I've heard," he said.

"Hello, Grace!" someone said behind me, and the first thing I knew I was talking to a lot of other people. When I looked around again for the young man from California, Mr. Ira Colton, maker of bright shiny gadgets, had him buttonholed. I didn't feel it was my duty to rescue him. He might, I thought, even persuade Mr. Colton that there really wasn't any promethium, and save him time and money, if not disappointment.

4

I WAS DINING WITH SOME FRIENDS— Elizabeth and Mac Bradley—on Massachusetts Avenue that night. It was a few minutes before eight when I entered their upstairs drawing room, but two other guests whom I knew were already there. My hosts were sitting in front of the fire with them.

"My dear, we were just scandal-mongering," Elizabeth said. She drew me down on the sofa beside her. "Have you heard about Stanley Woland?"

"His name's Wolanski," her husband said.

"I know, but you mustn't! He has a right to change his name if he wants to. Anyway, my dear, he went around to a woman who used to be very fond of him and borrowed five thousand dollars."

"She was a fool to let him have it."

"Oh, darling, please let me get on—he'll be here in a minute. . . . Oh, no, I don't mean Stanley; I mean the girl's uncle, Bartlett Folger. Anyway, Stanley told her he'd found this wealthy girl he was sure would marry him, and she was coming here to live and he had to get his car out of hock and put on a decent front, and, my dear, it's practically in the bag. All of us will be wishing we'd been nicer to Stanley before we're through."

"I won't," Mac said.

"Oh, well, you, darling. Nobody expects you to admit you were wrong about anything. But the point about it is that the Hilyard child—I can't think of her name —has turned down dozens of really splendid boys, all because she had a silly love affair with a workman in her father's plant. And now her mother's so relieved that she's delighted to have her marry Stanley if she wants to."

"I'd rather my daughter would marry the garbage collector," her husband said.

"Well, I wouldn't, frankly. Stanley has beautiful manners."

"Are you sure the Hilyard child is going to marry him?" I asked.

"I don't know how he'll ever pay back the five thousand dollars if she doesn't. He hasn't a penny of his own, and he must have had——"

My hostess stopped abruptly. "Sh-h—there's her uncle."

She went forward to greet him. "Isn't this delightful!"

I watched Bartlett Folger bow to her and shake hands with Mac. I could see what Agnes had meant in her letter. He was very attractive. His face was so suntanned that the other men looked as if they'd spent the winter underground, and his black hair was shot with just enough gray to make the gray look premature. He was rather hard-bitten someway, although he also looked as if he hadn't done any work for quite a while. I found myself wondering why Mac and Elizabeth were having him there to dinner. If Lawrason Hilyard and his wife had been there, too, I'd have understood it, because Mac was also a dollar-a-year man, acting as a co-ordinator of some kind between economic agencies.

Just then I heard Bartlett Folger say, "I'm sorry the Hilyards couldn't come. My brother-in-law can't get out much. They're running him ragged these days. I suppose you heard about the attack on him in the House this afternoon."

"It probably didn't bother him," Mac said.

Mr. Folger's jaw hardened. "On the contrary. He's sacrificed a good deal to come here, and he's not used to politics. He doesn't know how to take it."

"He'll learn," Elizabeth said cheerfully. She introduced him around until she came to me. "And Mrs. Latham . . . Mr. Folger."

"I've heard a good deal of you, Mrs. Latham," he said. We shook hands. His was very cold. I thought for a moment he wasn't going to like me much. I've seldom seen such a calmly scrutinizing appraisal of one dinner guest by another. If we'd met in a pawnshop I could have understood it.

Then suddenly he became amazingly affable.

"I understand I'm having the pleasure of dining with you Friday, Mrs. Latham," he said. "I didn't realize you were going to be here this evening too."

I may have been mistaken, but I got the impression that Mr. Folger thought it was rather clever of me to have arranged it all so neatly. I was so annoyed that I felt the color rise in my cheeks—which, from Mr. Folger's point of view, must have clinched it very nicely. He wouldn't know, of course, that Sgt. Phineas T. Buck has made me unduly sensitive about eligible bachelors; nor could I tell him, as I should have liked to do, that the dinner at my house was Colonel Primrose's idea, not mine. I was delighted when dinner was announced. Until I found myself seated next to Mr. Folger, anyway.

As a matter of fact, the dinner was very pleasant, or was, until somehow—I wasn't able to figure it out because I was talking to the man on my left when it began—somebody brought Stanley Woland's name into the conversation.

I was first aware of it when I heard Bartlett Folger saying calmly, "We're delighted, of course. Even if it doesn't last, it means she's got over a schoolgirl attachment her parents had to break off."

In the little silence that ensued, our hostess said brightly, "Well, of course, I always think it's really a shame——"

"To destroy love's young dream?" Mr. Folger interrupted with a smile. "I thought so myself. I was in

charge of the mill at the time, and I liked the boy."
He smiled again. "I could see the parents' point of
view. It would have been a little awkward, if you own
a town, to have your daughter's mother-in-law running
a roadside filling station and hot-dog stand. At least
my sister thought so." He put his wineglass down, his
face becoming serious again. "As a matter of fact, I'm
not sure it wouldn't have been better to have made the
best of it. Diane would have come to her senses. Or
they might even have made a go of it. It's always a
mistake, in my opinion, to make unnecessary enemies.
And they made two very bitter ones."

"Who?" I asked. It was none of my business, of
course, but I found myself, just then—no doubt quite
irrationally—on the side of the woman running the
service station.

"The boy," Mr. Folger said calmly, "and my niece.
Diane has never forgiven her parents, and I don't believe she ever will."

"How did you—I mean, how was it broken up?"
someone asked.

"We paid the boy off," Mr. Folger said equably.
"He was very decent about it. I thought we were going
to have trouble. He could have got a lot more if he'd
sat tight. But this is just personal history——"

I, for one, was glad when Elizabeth got up and we
went into the drawing room for coffee, leaving the men
to their cigars.

"Of course, the point is," Elizabeth said calmly,

"that the Hilyards have made a tremendous lot of money and the young man certainly knew it. Promethium is in enormous demand, and it sells for thirty-seven dollars a pound. Mac says if they hadn't spent a lot developing it that they have to get out, they could sell for around eighteen dollars and make a good profit. He had me buy some of their stock over the counter several years ago at three, and he made me sell it last fall at forty-five. It's around fifty now."

It was nearly eleven when we got up to go. Bartlett Folger went down the stairs with me.

"May I see you home, Mrs. Latham?" he asked.

"Thanks," I said. "I have my car." Then, for fear I'd been a little offhand, I added, "I'm looking forward to seeing you Friday."

"Nothing could keep me away, Mrs. Latham," he replied.

I opened my front door, went inside and stopped. Lilac, who's normally in bed at ten o'clock, came waddling out of the back sitting room. She gave me a non-committal look, opened the basement door and went downstairs. For a moment I thought perhaps Colonel Primrose had dropped by, though he was hardly in the habit of appearing at that time of night. I laid my wrap across the newel post and went along to see. At the door I stopped again, abruptly.

Diane Hilyard was calmly sitting there on the ottoman in front of the fire, in her stocking feet, drinking a cup of hot chocolate and eating a piece of bread and butter. She had on the same periwinkle sweater and skirt she'd worn that afternoon. Her tan-and-brown saddle shoes were drying on the hearth, her beaver coat and an old brown felt riding hat were lying on the sofa.

"I hope you don't mind my being here," she said. "Your maid said my shoes were wet and made me take them off. She said I was cold, and I guess I was. Would you like some chocolate? I'm sure there's some left." She took the lid off the Dresden pot and looked in. "No, I'm afraid I've drunk it all. I'm sorry."

"I don't want any anyway," I said.

She finished her chocolate and put the cup and saucer down on the tray.

"I suppose you'd like to go to bed, wouldn't you?" she asked, reaching for her shoes.

"Not particularly," I said. "It's early yet."

I sat down, looking at her. It was hard to imagine her as a bitter enemy of her parents, or for that matter to imagine her married to Stanley Woland, who'd borrowed five thousand dollars to see him through his courtship. She turned her head and stared silently into the fire.

After a moment, she said, "It's very cold outside, isn't it?"

"Yes," I said. "And you don't have to talk if you don't want to."

I looked at the clock. It was twenty-five minutes past

eleven. She must have been there some time already. Her shoes were quite dry. I began to wonder if her mother knew where she was, but I hesitated to ask her. We just sat there in silence. She started a little as the French clock over her head on the mantel daintily struck the half hour.

"It's such a mess at our house," she said.

There was something wistfully matter-of-fact about the way she said it that was rather shocking.

"Everybody is always in a stew about something," she went on after another little pause. "My sister and her husband came for dinner and sat like a couple of —of accusing images all through it. My father's upset and my mother's upset and the servants are upset. Finally they all went in the library and shut the door."

She drew a long breath, picked up her other shoe and started putting it on.

"I don't know what I've done now. It's always something I've done, when they have these family conferences. I thought I'd finally done something to please them, but I guess I was wrong." She looked up from her shoelaces. "Did you ever have everything you did be wrong?" she asked earnestly.

I shook my head as soon as I got the sentence unscrambled and saw what she meant. She sat there for a moment looking at me..

"Did you have an older sister?" she asked calmly.

"I had a lot of brothers," I said. "No sisters."

"You were lucky. Mother says I'm just spiteful and

—and jealous, and maybe I am—I don't know. But my sister's always done everything right. She never tore her clothes or fell down when she skated. She always liked the proper people and wrote her bread-and-butter letters on time. All her teachers liked her, so she never had to study. She married the proper young man and she dresses properly and has the proper people to dine. She's a great comfort to her parents and a pain in the neck to her sister Diane."

She giggled suddenly and her eyes, as dark as sapphires in the glow from the fire, lighted up irrepressibly for an instant.

"I'm horrible, really. Unnatural, mother says. And I suppose I am." She faded out again like the sound on the radio. "When I couldn't stick it any more at home, I used to go over and talk to Agnes Philips. She said you'd let me come here when we came to Washington. I didn't really mean to come tonight, but I couldn't stand it another minute, with all of them acting like cannibals. I had to get away. I went to a movie, but— well, it was about a girl marrying a man her father wanted her to, and—well, I couldn't stay any longer, so I thought you might be home———"

"I'm glad you came," I said. "I hope you'll always come. It doesn't matter whether I'm here or not. Lilac's always around somewhere."

"She's nice. I wish we had somebody like her at our house." She got up and picked up her coat. All of a sudden she sat down on the sofa. "You don't like Stanley, do you?" she asked abruptly.

"I . . . don't dislike Stanley," I answered. By this time I was prepared for her rather startling statements, so I wasn't taken aback at all. "I've known him a long time."

"I'm going to marry him. Did mother tell you? She's telling almost everybody she talks to."

I shook my head. "Is it . . . his idea, or yours?"

"Mine," she said calmly. "I suppose that's what the row's about tonight. My sister's mad as hops. She heard he'd borrowed some money so he could take me around."

I looked at her with amazement. It seemed to me that any girl would have hotly resented either the fact or the accusation, and especially this girl.

"And he did," she went on coolly. "That's what I like about him. He's perfectly honest. He hasn't any money and he's never worked in his life. His car didn't break down in front of our house. He wants to marry a girl with money, and he'd heard about me. He told me so himself. He borrowed some money from a woman he knows, just the way people borrow from banks to conduct other kinds of business."

"But, Diane!" I began.

"I know it sounds awful," she agreed placidly. "But, you see, the only difference between him and my brother-in-law is that Stanley's perfectly open and aboveboard about it. Do you think Carey would have fallen in love with Joan if her father had—had owned a filling station?"

She picked up her hat and put it on the back of her

head; her pale gold hair stuck up like a cherub's halo around the narrow brim.

"You see, I thought I was in love, once," she said. Her face was as expressionless as an ivory figurine's. "His name was Bowen Digges. He was supposed to be in love with me. We had all kinds of the most lovely plans. My family offered him twenty-five hundred dollars to go away somewhere else and never see me again. And he took it. I've hated him ever since. And mother and my sister and my father say I've got to marry; it isn't decent to be an old maid. So, very well, I'm going to marry. I decided that a long time ago. I decided I'd marry the first presentable man who came along and who didn't pretend my father's money was an obstacle he'd do his best to get over. Anyway, Stanley's very amusing, and my sister can't stand him."

"And that's what's commonly known as cutting off your nose to spite your face, my pet," I said.

She got up quickly. "Don't say that?" She was angry, and pretty close to tears.

"I think it's about time somebody said it," I returned. "After all, your Bowen Digges and Stanley Woland are only two men out of an awful lot of extremely nice ones in the world."

"Then why haven't you ever married again?" she demanded.

"That's quite different," I said. "I've got two sons. Stepfathers——"

"Bowen and I were going to have six children," she

said quietly. "We were going to—we were going to do lots of things." She went over to the door. "Good-by."

"Wait a minute," I said. "Have you got a car?"

She shook her head. "I walked."

"Then I'll take you home. Don't be silly; you can't wander around the streets alone this time of night."

I put on my galoshes and coat and followed her out to the car. It had started to snow again. We sat there for a moment, waiting for the defroster to unstick the snow around the windshield wipers. Diane huddled down in the corner of the seat beside me, a silent furry bundle, her head bent forward in her coat collar, her hands stuck down in her pockets. She didn't move as I crossed Wisconsin Avenue and went cautiously along P Street as far as the university. I turned left and went along N to 37th, and down to Prospect Street.

The Hilyards' house was dark, except for the yellow half circle of the fanlight above the door. A party was just breaking up at a house a little way along, and the people were coming out and starting up their cars. There was no place to park in front of the Hilyards', so I stopped in the middle of the street, my headlights shining across the sidewalk and up the steps.

Diane took her hands out of her pockets and raised her head. She sat quite still for a moment. Then she said, "I feel better than I did. Thanks a lot. Good night—is it all right for me to call you Grace?"

"Of course," I said. "Good night, Diane. Don't do anything just to spite somebody—your sister, or your parents, or Bowen. Life's got too much in it, and you're much too sweet."

She shook her head slowly. "I think it's a first-class mess, myself. What I've seen of it." She put out her hand and pressed mine. "Oh, I'm not so bad as I sound, actually. Thanks anyway, Grace. Good night." She opened the door and slid out onto the snowy street.

"Be careful you don't slip," I said.

A man in dinner jacket and overcoat was coming along, his head down against the snow. He had a dark-haired girl in a long white dress by the arm, and they were laughing and sliding along the slippery walk, headed for the car in front of the Hilyards'. I waited with my foot on the brake as Diane went over to the sidewalk and stepped up on the curb. And just as she cleared it her feet went out from under her and down she went.

"Oh, damn!" she said. She was half laughing and half mad, but not at all hurt.

I got out of the car, but before I got to the curb, the man coming along had dropped the girl's arm and jumped forward to help Diane up.

"Upsy-daisy!" he said. They were all three of them laughing, and so was I. He pulled Diane up to her feet. And suddenly he dropped her arms, and they just stood there, staring at each other. I stopped where I was and stared too.

Diane raised her hand slowly and touched his face with her finger tips.

"Bo," she whispered. "Bo."

The second time it was a low cry from somewhere very deep inside her. She moved her eyes slowly from him to the girl in the white evening frock standing a little to one side in the bright glare of my headlights. Then she looked back at him, at the starched front of his dinner shirt and the black silk lapels of his jacket. Her face was blank and white and stunned. And so, I imagine, was mine.

The young man standing there was Bowen Digges. He was also the same young man from OPM that I'd talked to in the corner behind the piano at the party that afternoon—the young man from California who didn't know Diane's sister and brother-in-law socially, but knew their names, and whose boss was Lawrason Hilyard, and who'd said—it came back to me in a sudden flash—that he hated Lawrason Hilyard's guts.

He was standing there quite calmly. I could hear myself that afternoon saying, "There's another daughter. She's beautiful," and hear him answering me, "So I've heard."

For a minute something odd seemed to happen to his face, as if he had a slow pain inside him. He started to move, and caught himself sharply. A twisted sort of grin came to his face.

"You're right, Miss Hilyard," he said. "I've got dinner clothes now. But my mother still used to run a roadside store."

Diane stared at him as if he'd slapped her in the

face, her jaw dropping a little, her eyes as blankly un-understanding as a child's.

"I hope you didn't hurt yourself," he said. "May I——"

She turned and ran. Why she didn't slip and fall again, I'll never know. She was up the steps, knocking frantically on the door. It opened suddenly. Her father stood there under the hall light. She stumbled forward and past him.

He turned and stared after her, and then looked back out into the street. I saw his hand drop from the knob as he recognized Bowen Digges.

"Good evening, sir," Bowen said.

Mr. Hilyard nodded curtly and closed the door.

"Well, of all things," the girl in the white dress said. "Who was that?"

"That," Bowen Digges said, "was a girl I used to know. Be careful you don't slip, and look out for your skirt."

I went back to my car. I don't think he'd even seen me, and I was sure he hadn't recognized me if he had. He waited till I got my car started and out of his way. I heard his motor go on and race violently for a moment behind me.

It just didn't make sense, I thought. He'd never been "paid off" by any two thousand, five hundred dollars. I would have been willing to stake everything I owned on that. There was some ghastly mistake somewhere. I'd as soon have believed one of my own sons had done such a thing. They just weren't that kind of people.

That was Monday night at half past twelve. It was on Tuesday night at eleven thirty-five that Lawrason Hilyard's watch stopped when he fell or was thrown into the Georgetown Canal. And as far as anyone knew or could find out, Bowen Digges was the last person who had seen him alive.

5

LILAC PUT THE WEDNESDAY MORNING papers on my bed and went over to close the windows. I knew by the way she slammed them down that something was wrong. I looked at the clock on the table. It was twenty-five minutes past seven. As I have breakfast at eight, that meant something was very wrong indeed; but since I'm well used to the kind of things that make Lilac revert practically to the jungle, I just took a deep breath, sat up and waited. She came back to the foot of the bed.

"Did you read what it says in there?" she demanded. I could almost hear the tom-toms beat in the tone of her voice.

I picked the paper up. All I saw was war and more war.

"Down at th' bottom," she said.

I glanced down at an item in a box at the lower-left-hand corner. The type was heavy, indicating that it was last-minute news.

"Well-dressed man believed suicide," it said. "The body of a well-dressed man was removed from the

Chesapeake and Ohio Canal early this morning. The man was five feet, eleven and one half inches tall, had graying hair, wore a gray suit with a gray striped shirt and a green-figured tie bought at a Washington store. No identifying papers were found. The body was removed to the morgue at Gallinger Hospital pending police investigation."

I looked up at Lilac blankly.

"That's him, all right," she said.

"Who?" I demanded. "What on earth are you talking about?"

"Mist' Hilyer," she said flatly. "Boston, he's downstairs right this minute. He says it's Mist' Hilyer. He says he ain' goin' back to that house. Ain' nobody goin' to make him go back neither."

I forced myself to be a lot calmer than I was.

"What makes Boston think it's Mr. Hilyard?"

"Boston don' think, he know," she said angrily. "Mist' Hilyer ain' come home at all las' night. He come in jus' 'fore eleven an' started raisin' time 'cause Boston he wouldn' go out in the dark with that dog they got. He had somebody in his study, an' they took th' dog out theirselves. Th' dog come back wringin' wet, but Mist' Hilyer he never come, an' he ain' come yet. Boston ain' goin' back neither. An' Ah don' blame him."

I just sat there staring at her for an instant. "Does Mrs. Hilyard know it?" I asked then.

"Boston ain' said nothin'. He ain' seen her. He got

th' paper an' he come straight over here. It don' surprise him none."

"All right, Lilac," I said. "Now just be quiet and put my breakfast on a tray downstairs. I'll get up."

I waited until I heard her going down the stairs, and then I reached over and dialed Colonel Primrose's number. He answered the phone himself.

"This is Grace Latham, colonel," I said quickly. "They found a man's body in the canal this morning; it's in the paper. Boston say it's Mr. Hilyard."

I caught a kind of sharpened silence at the other end of the line.

"He's their butler. He's over here now with Lilac."

"What makes him think it's Hilyard?" Colonel Primrose asked calmly. It's wonderful never to be jolted out of the even tenor of your way.

"The description," I said. Having asked the same question myself, I suppose it was silly of me to be irritated by Colonel Primrose's asking it. "Plus the fact that Mr. Hilyard didn't come home last night. The body's at the morgue. I gather Mrs. Hilyard doesn't even know he's not home. You might do something about it."

"I will, at once," he said imperturbably. "Thanks for calling. I'll let you know about it as soon as I can."

I took a shower and got dressed quickly. I was really much more upset about it than actually I had any cause to be, or than I would have been if Diane hadn't dried her shoes in front of my fire, or if the young man at

the cocktail party hadn't turned out to be Bowen Digges,
After all, people have to die, and if they choose to
commit suicide, it's their own business. The idea that
it was murder didn't enter my head.

All the time I was dressing I kept seeing Mr. Hilyard standing in the door under the fanlight, looking
first at his daughter stumbling along the hall and then
back at Bowen Digges standing there on the sidewalk
in the glare of my headlights, and I kept hearing
Bowen Digges say, "That was a girl I used to know."
And it was all very puzzling. Hilyard had known for
three months that the man they'd said he'd paid to get
rid of was there in Washington, sitting in the same office with him. He must have realized that sooner or
later he and Diane couldn't help but meet. Washington
has got awfully big, but it's not that big yet. And then
it struck me suddenly. Maybe that was why he was
going to resign—if his wife had been telling me the
truth. But if that was the reason, he would never have
let Diane come on in the first place. It didn't make
sense, I thought.

Agnes Philips had said that Lawrason Hilyard was
a ruthless man. Ruthless men don't resign major jobs
just because old beaus of their daughters unexpectedly
turn up in responsible positions owning dinner jackets.
And they certainly don't kill themselves for that reason.

Nevertheless, I thought, I'd like to have known
what went on in the Hilyard household the day after
Diane met and recognized Bowen Digges. She had come

over, as a matter of fact, when I was out, and stayed a couple of hours. I managed to phone her before I went out to dinner, but she was out then, so that I hadn't even talked to her since the street scene of Monday night. I regretted it now much more than I had before.

I sat down at my breakfast tray, picked up the paper again, and settled down to wait for Colonel Primrose's call. I glanced at the item at the bottom of the front page, and turned to the inside. RUMORS OF OPM SHAKE-UP was the first thing that caught my eye. I read through the story carefully.

"As a result of recent airings of the promethium situation in the House of Representatives, the corridors of the Social Security Building are rife with speculation as to a possible shift in control," it said. "The best bet as to a likely successor to Lawrason Hilyard, present branch chief, is Bowen Digges, now assistant to Mr. Hilyard. He is regarded as an exceptionally able addition to the younger ranks of the Office of Production Management, and also considered highly acceptable to the congressional bloc that has been a thorn in the side of the dollar-a-year men. Digges came directly from the California Institute of Technology and has a broad knowledge of war needs and the available supply of the critical so-called 'magic metal.' Only twenty-eight years old, he has had experience in the practical as well as the academic and theoretical field of metallurgy. He is energetic and likable, is given much of the credit for the speed with which the limited supply of promethium has found its way into military essentials, and is said to have been responsible for the vigorous curtailment of nondefense use of the metal and a generous absence of red tape and delay. If a shake-up comes, his appointment will meet with enthusiasm, especially in Army and Navy procurement circles."

I went through it a second time. It seemed to me one of the most ironic commentaries I'd ever read. The man that Lawrason Hilyard didn't think was good enough to marry his daughter was being credited with the success of her father's job and spoken of as his successor. The fact that his mother had run a roadside store and service station was a factor of no importance.

I put the paper down. What if—but that didn't make sense. Lawrason Hilyard wouldn't conceivably go out and kill himself because Bowen Digges was going to supersede him. It might be hard to take, but not that hard.

I glanced on through the paper until I came to the pictures on the back page. SOCIETY DANCES FOR SAVE THE CHILDREN, I read. The middle picture showed Diane Hilyard in a white lace ballerina frock and silver-fox jacket, laughing up at Stanley Woland, resplendent in white tie and tails with a topper in his hand. Under it was the head, WEDDING BELLS?

"Neither the former Count Stanislaus Wolanski, who recently dropped his title, nor the glamorous newcomer to Capitol society, Diane Hilyard, would deny or confirm it," it went on. "They are seen here arriving at the ball. Miss Hilyard is the younger daughter of Lawrason Hilyard, OPM executive."

I looked intently at Diane's radiant face, incredibly lovely even in the startling flare of the flashlight photograph. There was nothing in it by which I could recognize the stunned stricken child who had stumbled past her father into the hall on Monday night. Certainly not the dazzling laughter in it, I thought, and arriving at benefit balls in Washington hotels isn't that much fun —not with a man you aren't in love with, anyway.

I put the paper down and finished my cold coffee and toast. Sheila, my Irish setter, raised her head from her paws and growled just then, just before the doorbell rang and Lilac came padding up the steps to answer it. In a moment Colonel Primrose came in.

I saw at once, from the look on his face, that there wasn't any doubt the man they'd found in the Chesapeake and Ohio Canal was Lawrason Hilyard. Boston was right.

Colonel Primrose nodded. "Bartlett Folger identified him."

"Was it suicide?"

"It looks that way. Folger doesn't believe it. He chucked his weight about a good deal. Hilyard wasn't the sort to do away with himself, in the first place, and if he'd decided to shoot himself——"

"Shoot himself?" I said. "My paper didn't——"

"I know. The police phoned the papers. There weren't any reporters around when he was brought in.

But shot he was. Folger thinks if he was going to shoot himself he'd have done it at home, or in a hotel room, not tramp two miles to do it in the snow on the bank of a canal. There's something in it."

"Then he thinks——"

I stopped. After the conversation at dinner Monday night, it was fairly obvious what Mr. Bartlett Folger must have thought.

"He hasn't said it in so many words—the implication is clear enough," Colonel Primrose answered. "And it's going to be hard to prove, with half of Precinct Seven tramping over the ground. They found his gun there by the body."

"Will the police do anything about it?"

He smiled wryly. "Very much so. Folger made it perfectly plain. It has to be thoroughly cleared up or else."

"Or else what?"

"He'd get somebody down from New York on his own. After all the missiles the police have had thrown at them the last six months, they'll do all they can. You remember Lamb, don't you?"

I nodded. I remembered Captain Lamb very well. He is chief of the Homicide Squad, and an able man.

"He was on hand this morning. I phoned him as soon as you called. He's gone down to the canal now, and I'm joining him. If you'd like to come along——"

I suppose I shouldn't have jumped up as eagerly as I did, because he gave me a sardonic smile.

"What's your interest in this, Mrs. Latham?" he inquired placidly. "I think you'd better tell me about your call Monday afternoon. I tried to get hold of you all day yesterday."

"They were coming to dinner Friday," I said. "All of them. I'll go get my coat."

"You'd better change your shoes too. We're going to do some walking. It's a couple of miles from the Thirty-sixth Street Bridge."

I put on some heavy walking shoes and wool socks and came downstairs again. Sheila, spotting my shoes and knowing that meant she was going for a walk, went to the front door and began to paw it impatiently.

"You can't go, miss," I said.

Her face fell. She looked up at Colonel Primrose.

"Why don't we take her?" he said. "She can have a good run before we get there."

She was out with a bound, when I opened the door, and over to the car.

"Where's Sergeant Buck?" I asked. The icy bricks of the sidewalk must have reminded me of him.

"Down there with Lamb," Colonel Primrose said. "I wish you two got along better."

"If you'd just explain to him that I'm not trying to marry you, we'd get along fine," I said.

"But think what a blow that would be to my ego."

"Then let's skip it, by all means. Did you hear about the man who's been hanging around the Hilyards' house?"

He shook his head. "Tell me."

"I'll tell you if you'll find out about it yourself, without involving me in it," I said.

"Considering that I've wasted the greater part of the last few years trying to keep you from involving yourself in trouble of various kinds," Colonel Primrose said blandly, "it's a pleasure to have you have such an idea. Go on. I want the whole thing, Mrs. Latham."

6

WE'D COME, BY THE TIME I'D TOLD HIM,
to the iron bridge across the canal at the end of the old
Arlington Aqueduct below the Key Bridge, in front of
the big red-brick building of the traction company on M
Street.

Sheila bounded out of the car as soon as I parked,
and shot past the policeman on guard and down the
steps to the towing path. Colonel Primrose showed his
card, and we crossed over after her.

I'd better explain that the Chesapeake and Ohio
Canal is about eighty feet wide, with a retaining wall
along M Street and Canal Road as far as the Chain
Bridge. The towing path, about ten feet wide, is on the
river side, and there's quite a stretch of land, including
a railroad track and fishing and boating places, between
it and the Potomac.

The canal took the place of an earlier one that
George Washington was interested in, and was begun in
1828. It was the water route to Cumberland from the
point in Georgetown where the river became non-nav-
igable because of rocks and falls and shallows. It was

given up, eventually, for better modes of transportation, and fell into ruin until the National Park Service took it over a few years ago. Now it's a delightful place, very beautiful along the banks of the river, and the pleasantest place in the world to take a dog to run. Sheila knows every molehill and every rabbit hole along it.

The ground along the towing path was frozen now, with a few late violets still sticking their pale frozen faces out from under sheltering leaves. Colonel Primrose and I followed Sheila along. I told him as much of what I knew about the Hilyards as I thought I had to and that he'd find out from somebody else anyway and know I'd purposely held back. Otherwise I wouldn't have said anything about Mr. Bartlett Folger's conversation at dinner Monday night. I left out most of my conversation with Bowen Digges at the cocktail party, except to say there'd been one and that I liked Bowen Digges even before I knew who he was. I also left out most of what Diane had said, except that the household had been pretty much upset that night.

"I suppose Carey and Joan Eaton recognized Digges, and that's what the trouble was about," Colonel Primrose remarked.

I don't know why I hadn't thought of that myself, but I hadn't, somehow. It explained, of course, why Joan Eaton had stared at the two of us, in the corner there by the piano, and why her husband had taken such elaborate care not to be seen looking at us. I'd still connected that vaguely with the radio incident outside the front door. And it meant, of course, that they hadn't known he was in her father's office either.

"I'd like to know about Bowen Digges," I said. "How do you suppose he got from washer-up in the plant laboratory—isn't that what Agnes said he was?—to runner-up for Mr. Hilyard's job as OPM branch chief in five years?"

"It would be interesting to find out," he said. His voice came from a curious angle. I looked around. He was no longer directly behind me on the path; he'd stopped and was bending down to look at something in the tangled vines to our left. Monday's snow was still fairly heavy on the ground among the roots, but it had melted off the upper layer of leafless runners, now shaggy white with hoarfrost from the night before.

He straightened up, holding an empty cigarette packet between his thumb and forefinger by the torn blue revenue label. Whoever had tossed it away had apparently given it a twist in the midde first. It was covered with frost too. Colonel Primrose unbuttoned his overcoat and dropped it into his suit-coat pocket.

"Now, really, Colonel Primrose!" I said.

He chuckled. "You can't ever tell," he said calmly.

We'd come along the towing path a little more than a mile—we measured it later on my speedometer on the Canal Road, across the canal beyond the stone retaining wall. The twisted cigarette pack was directly across from the broken place in the wall just past Clark

Place Road, and exactly a mile and one tenth from the green iron bridge at the foot of the long flight of cement steps from Prospect Street down to M Street. And it was three quarters of a mile farther along, that Lawrason Hilyard's body had been found.

We came in sight of the place in a few minutes, around a long even bend of the canal. A crowd of dark-coated figures were milling about. Somebody had built a fire, and the smoke made a lovely mauve haze above them.

"They must have put half the force on the job," I said.

Colonel Primrose groaned audibly. "Everything will be churned to mush," he said.

We went on. There were a lot of cars up on the road across the canal. A battery of cameramen were sitting or standing on the retaining wall. One was weaving up a big bare overhanging sycamore like a monkey. I could hear the shrill blast of a police whistle farther along, where a policeman was diverting traffic from the Virginia shore up the Chain Bridge Road. The identity of the dead man was pretty obviously known by now, and the press was out in full cry.

Colonel Primrose took my arm. We quickened our pace.

"You think he was murdered, don't you?" I asked.

He looked around at me. "I don't know, Mrs. Latham. If he was, I'd like to know why. And if it's suicide, I'd still like to know why. I was a fool to let

Lamb get here ahead of me. The trouble with the Washington police just now is that they're scared to death of the press. They're like a lot of prima donnas."

He was certainly right in part. The whole bank of the canal, as we got up to the milling crowd there, was trampled to liquid mud. A couple of reporters spotted him and came running to meet us.

"Hi, colonel! What's the dope?"

"You tell me. I've just come."

"Tell us another, colonel. What's Captain Lamb doing here? And your man Friday?"

Colonel Primrose's man Friday made the weather seem much warmer all of a sudden. He was standing there, his back to the canal, a frozen colossus athwart the one piece of untrodden ground visible. I looked down at it as we came up. Between his feet a dark brown scum oozed through the dead water irises and stained the snow on the bank.

"Stand back," Captain Lamb said. "Get back, all you fellows. . . . His feet were up here," he went on as Colonel Primrose came to a stop there. "His body was in up to the waist."

He pointed out into the fringe of brown-stained water plants. The water was still muddy. The shallow rim of ice along the canal bank was broken and slowly forming again.

Captain Lamb motioned to a shivering, unattractive little man in an old trench coat. "Come out here, you, and tell the colonel what you told me. . . . This is the fellow that found him, colonel. . . . And what were you doing down here?"

The little man came forward serenely.

"It's a national park, ain't it? I've got a right to go on a picnic, like anybody else?"

"Get on with it, please," Colonel Primrose said.

"Okay. My name's Andrews. I spent the night in that shack down there. I didn't break in—the door wasn't locked. I was waked up by a pistol shot. It was dark and I don't know what time it was—I left my watch in my other pants. A dog was barking up here. He barked and howled till I thought I'd get up and see what was going on. There was a flashlight in the cupboard. I came up here, and first thing I saw this guy in the water with a little dog tugging at his leg. I had to chase it off before I could get hold of him and pull him out. First I thought I'd yell when a car came along, and then I figured the first thing they'd do would be nab me. Anyway, the guy was dead, and he wouldn't be any colder layin' here than on a slab in the morgue. So I just left him where he was. I went to Georgetown and got a cup of coffee. I sat there gassin' with the Greek that runs the place till I got feelin' sorry for the guy out here. I went to the call box and waited for the cop to come."

Colonel Primrose nodded. "All right. . . . Lamb, get everybody out of here, onto the other side. I want to have a look. . . . Sorry, boys."

The newspapermen were good-natured about it. It

was a long trek back and around, I was thinking, but they were smarter than that. They went up the canal about fifty feet to a skiff moored to the bank. It was tied by two long ropes, one fast to a cement pile in the back, the other to the foot of a short flight of steps down to the water across the canal, by an iron gate in the wall, so that the boat could be pulled back and forth to either side. In a moment Colonel Primrose and Sergeant Buck, Captain Lamb, the little tramp, a policeman, a detective and I were the only ones left on the towing path.

"Where was his gun?" Colonel Primrose asked.

The little tramp pointed down. "Just here. Left of the body. He was lying on his face. I turned him over when I pulled him out, to see if his heart was beating. His face was all covered with mud. That's why I didn't see that he had a hole in his head."

Colonel Primrose turned to the uniformed policeman. "You took the body up?"

"Yes, sir. I put in a call for the wagon and came down here with this man. I spotted that boat up there and carried the body up and put it in, and the boys on the other side pulled it across and took it away."

Just at that moment the low wail of a siren came through the air like the call of a lost banshee. The policeman stopped short, we all looked around. A motorcycle escorting a green coupé swept up Canal Road from Georgetown and came to a dramatic stop under the naked ghost-white sycamores beyond the wall. A door opened and slammed shut.

The next instant I saw the group of men up there on the road fall apart and a sudden spot of gold light the bleak landscape.

Diane Hilyard ran to the wall. Her face, as she stood a moment poised above the wall, her hands gripping the gray stone, looking across at the towing path, was so white that it didn't look real. The men there stood sort of paralyzed for an instant. Then there was a shout of recognition, and a dozen cameras were whipped up and began to click like mad.

Colonel Primrose glanced at me. I nodded.

"It's Miss Hilyard, Lamb," he said curtly. "Bring her across. Get her away from those fools."

Diane had seen the steps down and the boat. She ran past the policeman there, her bright bob pushed back, her beaver coat open. The policeman stood aside as Captain Lamb bellowed something. She ran down the rickety wooden steps and stumbled into the skiff. It was Sergeant Buck who strode up to the mooring and pulled her across. I ran along the path to her just as he was practically lifting her out.

I could forgive Sergeant Buck everything in the past, I thought, for the genuine compassion in that lantern-jawed dead pan of his just then. He was patting her shoulder awkwardly.

"There, there, miss. There, there, now." It was a hoarse croak, coming out of the corner of his brass-bound mouth, but it sounded unbelievably sweet. "Now, now, miss; it'll be all right."

He shot me a look of almost pathetic appeal, and

nodded at the skiff. I looked down at it. It was a horrible sickening mess, with the stained, awful water sloshing about the flat, uneven bottom around the cleats. It was the boat, of course, I realized, in which they'd taken Lawrason Hilyard's body across.

I took hold of her arm. "Come along, Diane," I said gently.

She turned to me. Her face was completely bloodless. Her scarlet lipstick stood out as if it were painted on white linen. Her eyes were perfectly dry and as blue as cobalt if cobalt could be made to feel. Her whole body was quivering.

"It was my father, Grace," she whispered, as if she didn't know I knew.

"I know, darling," I said.

"But, Grace! How could it happen?"

"I don't know, Diane," I said. "But why did you come? Why don't you go back home?"

She seemed to straighten up, and her hand in mine stopped trembling. "I had to. Boston came back. He said he'd been at your house, and you'd come here with somebody called Colonel Primrose."

I nodded.

"Where is he?"

"Down there."

As she started forward, Sergeant Buck cleared his throat. When Sergeant Buck clears his throat, everybody stops. It sounds like a *Panzer* division going through a mountain ravine, and there's a compelling note of authority in it that I, for one, would hesitate to disregard. We both stopped and turned. Sergeant Buck gets the color of tarnished brass when he's embarrassed. He was that color now.

"I just wanted to say I'd take care what I said, miss," he said. "The colonel don't mean any harm. But I'd watch my step all the same."

A look of alarm flashed across Diane's face. She turned back to me, her lips parted. Boston, I gathered, had put Colonel Primrose one notch above the cherubim in what Sergeant Buck calls the "hy-rarchy"—though he uses the word only about the Administration setup —and she'd believed him.

"Oh, dear," she said. "I thought——"

Sergeant Buck's face went a shade more granite. "Don't say nothing without due consideration," he said.

"He means that the police are here too," I put in. "And reporters."

I knew that wasn't what he meant in the least, and that what he meant was exactly what he'd said. What puzzled me was why he'd said it—for he must have known much more about what was in his colonel's mind than I did. Perhaps it was just as well he did, for Diane didn't rush down the path impulsively, as it seemed she was going to do at first. She went along quietly and stopped, looking at the colonel and Captain Lamb and the little tramp huddled there by the smoking embers.

I introduced her.

"I just came to say that you mustn't believe them, Colonel Primrose, when they say my father . . . took his own life," she said. "He wouldn't do such a thing. He had contempt for . . . weakness of any sort." She looked around her. "And he wouldn't come out here to a place like this, if he was doing it!" she cried suddenly. "Never! Never! You've got to find out who did it!"

Captain Lamb spoke, "Did your father have any——"

I'm sure he was going to say, ". . . enemies that you know of, miss?" It's always his first question, and the answer is always "No," but he keeps on asking it. He didn't finish this time, for there was a sharp flurry in the underbrush just off the railroad tracks on the other side of the towing path. I could see my red setter's tail waving, and hear her barking in sharp, excited little yelps. The next instant she was bounding across the tracks. In her mouth she had a dark gray object. The policeman made a dive at her as she came up, but she dodged him playfully and came over to me.

"What's that?" Captain Lamb asked.

"It appears to be a man's hat," I said. I took it from her. It was one of those soft sport things that can be rolled up and poked out again without losing whatever shape they had to begin with. I unrolled it and held it out gingerly. There was a dark, frozen bloodstain on the brim. I looked inside at the sweatband.

"Your father's, Miss Hilyard?" Captain Lamb said.

Diane, standing beside me, was looking at the leather

band too. I knew it without even glancing toward her. It was one of the most interminable fractions of a moment that I've ever spent. She put her hand out and took it.

"Yes," she said. "That's my father's. May I have it? You don't need it, do you?"

Captain Lamb nodded. "I guess it's all right. Only I'd like to know how it got over there."

The little tramp spoke up, "I put it over there. It was layin' here on the grass. I didn't see how he'd be usin' it any more."

Captain Lamb turned on him with some annoyance, I thought. "Anything else you got hidden around here?"

I didn't hear what else was said. The tumult in my mind was deafening. I was trying desperately to concentrate on being casual, so that Colonel Primrose wouldn't know. Because the hat was not Lawrason Hilyard's. The initials on the sweatband were "B.D.," and the merchant's label said College Toggery. Pasadena, California.

Diane Hilyard had told a deliberate lie. And she'd done it so convincingly that not even Colonel Primrose suspected it. He was so concerned with the tramp that he hadn't paid any attention to either of us.

7

LAWRASON HILYARD HAD NOT BEEN BROUGHT
back to the house in Prospect Street, but Death was
there. He was at the closed door and at the shuttered
windows. His sable shadow lay cold in the silent hall.

I came back with Diane. I didn't want to, and my
heart sank as we came in. She held onto my hand.

"Please don't go," she whispered. "You've got to
help me. At least stay till they go."

She meant Colonel Primrose and Captain Lamb,
coming along later. Sergeant Buck was taking Sheila
home in my car. I listened. The sound of low voices
was coming from the library, and from somewhere upstairs the sound of hysterical weeping.

"What am I going to do with this?"

Diane pulled the bloodstained hat out of her pocket.
A chair moved in the library; the brass knob turned.
She thrust the hat into my hand just as the door
opened. The young man I'd seen at the cocktail party,
Carey Eaton, her sister's husband, came into the hall.

"Where have you been all———"

He saw me behind her in the shadowy hall and
stopped abruptly, his face flushing. I got the hat into

my own pocket as he came towards us, his feet sharp on the waxed floor. He had every reason to object to my being there, of course, and I didn't blame him. It did seem a little odd that he should have been speaking to Diane as he was.

"Everybody's been hunting you all over the place, Diane," he said curtly. "I should think you'd at least have enough respect for your father's——"

"Oh, shut up!" Diane cried. She flared up for an instant like a rocket, and subsided as quickly. "I'm sorry, Carey, but please don't go on like that. I can't stand any more."

"All I'm saying is that your mother——"

"I know. Please don't. I shouldn't have gone out. I'm sorry."

"And who is this you've brought here?" He gave me as cold a stare as I deserved. "I should think——"

She cut him off abruptly. "This is Mrs. Latham . . . my brother-in-law, Mr. Eaton. She came because I asked her to. Because the police are on their way here now."

Carey Eaton took another step toward us. "The police?" he began angrily. "What have you been doing? Where——"

The library door opened again. It was Mr. Bartlett Folger. He looked gray and at least ten years older than he had Monday night at dinner.

"For God's sake, Carey——" He stopped short, staring at me.

"Diane's brought the police here!" Carey Eaton said violently. "I told you all that was what she'd do! I'd like to——"

Bartlett Folger stepped quickly across the hall and took him by the arm. "Be quiet, Carey," he said sharply. His face was white with anger. "You're acting like a fool." He turned to me. "I'm sorry, Mrs. Latham. Lawrason's death has upset everybody. Is there something——"

"Mrs. Latham came because I asked her to, Uncle Bart," Diane said calmly. "I had an idea that if there was a stranger in the house, the Eatons would behave like civilized white people. I also thought I'd like to have a friend."

I turned as another door opened and Mrs. Hilyard came into the hall. I'd thought it was she who was crying upstairs, but it wasn't. She was by far the calmest and most self-possessed of the family. Her face above her unrelieved black dress was chalky white, and there were darkish circles under her eyes, but she was in complete command of herself and the situation thrust upon her. "Thank you for coming, Mrs. Latham," she said quietly. "I appreciate it very deeply."

She held out her hand. I felt like a yellow dog. I wasn't there in any sense of condolence or sympathy. I mumbled something or other, and she pressed my hand quickly.

"I know it's very hard to know what to say," she said. She turned to her daughter. "Go upstairs, Diane, and take off those wet shoes. And change into something a little more suitable, won't you, please, dear?"

Diane looked down at her muddy feet. The color rose to her cheeks. She shot a defiant glance at her brother-in-law and left.

Her mother drew a deep, wavering breath and turned back to me. She was making a definite effort to keep her voice steady.

"Will you come in and talk to me a minute? . . . And please, Carey, try to be more tactful with Diane. I can't endure any more of this. . . . Bartlett, go up and talk to her, please. Try to do something with her."

She closed the library door behind us and stood leaning back against it for a moment with her eyes closed.

"Diane doesn't mean to make everything so difficult," she said, coming over to me and sitting down. Then she said "Oh, dear!" and got up quickly.

I hadn't meant to stare, but I suppose I must have done so.

An antique pearwood armchair that I'd heard Mrs. Ralston call one of her museum pieces was now in about fifteen pieces in the corner between the Chippendale kneehole desk and the corner windows.

Mrs. Hilyard went to the fireplace and pulled the bell cord.

"I didn't want Mrs. Ralston to leave it here; it's so old and fragile," she said, looking down at the heap of old wood and needle point. "My brother sat on it and it literally came to pieces."

"It can be mended," I said, though I didn't see how anybody just sitting on it could break it that way. It looked much more as if it had been picked up and slammed down.

"Put that chair in the hall closet, please, Boston," Mrs. Hilyard said.

"Mr. Folger, he tol' me not to touch it, ma'am," Boston said. "He say to leave it where it is."

She cut him off sharply. "I say to move it." There were two dull spots of color in her cheeks that hadn't been there before.

"Yes, ma'am."

He gathered the pieces hastily and got out. He hadn't even glanced at me. He wasn't very happy. His skin had that funny color they get—a sort of mixture of lampblack and white lead and yellow ocher.

"I wish you would help me with Diane, Mrs. Latham," Mrs. Hilyard said. She sat down beside me again. "I'm so worried about her that I'm almost out of my mind."

"I think she's very sweet," I said. "I gather she's rather headstrong, but——"

That was as far as we got on the subject of Diane. Boston was at the door again.

"The police are coming, ma'am," he said to Mrs. Hilyard breathlessly. "They're getting out of the car."

"Show them in when they come, Boston. And ask Mr. Folger and the others to come down."

I heard that deeply drawn, wavering breath again.

Otherwise she was calm enough, though I had the idea that she hadn't planned it this way.

"I hope you'll forgive us, Mrs. Latham," she said. "We're all on the ragged edge."

And they were, though they did manage to pull themselves together when Colonel Primrose and Captain Lamb finally came in. Where those two had been from the time Boston announced their arrival until almost fifteen minutes later, when the doorbell rang and Bartlett Folger went to let them in himself, I couldn't imagine.

It was an extraordinary situation. Mr. Folger had come down first, then Joan and Carey Eaton. Joan's eyes were red and swollen, and the powder she'd hastily dabbed on to try to cover up the mottled tearstains on her cheeks had dried unevenly. Her husband sat down beside her—I thought as nervous as an ill-tempered cat. Bartlett Folger paced up and down. Finally Diane came down. She looked around.

"I thought Carey said the police had come," she said calmly.

Her brother-in-law's retort was cut shot by the peal of the doorbell. "There they are now," he said. "For God's sake, Diane——"

"Be quiet, Carey," Mrs. Hilyard said sharply. "If you're going to act like this, I wish you'd go upstairs. You're not the head of this house yet."

There was an abrupt tight silence when Mr. Folger introduced Colonel Primrose. I had the feeling—and it wasn't the first time I'd had it in situations of the sort—that someone in the room hadn't counted on anyone like him coming in. They had—one of them, or all of them, I couldn't tell—expected a professional policeman like Captain Lamb; they had not expected anyone as completely at ease in the well-bred elegance of the Ralston library as they themselves were. Or rather more than they were just then, I thought, except for Diane, who already knew about him.

"When I spoke to you this morning, captain," Bartlett Folger said, rather abruptly, "I told you the idea of suicide was absurd. Since I've talked with my sister, I want to withdraw that."

Colonel Primrose looked over at Mrs. Hilyard. "Why do you think your husband might have taken his own life?" he asked.

"He threatened to do so several times recently," she said. "I've lived in constant dread of it." Her voice was steady, but it seemed to take all the effort she was capable of to keep it that way. "He's been horribly upset lately, and working much too hard. His stomach has been bothering him so that he's been going to the doctor for the first time in his life. As soon as I found out that he hadn't come home last night, I went to his desk drawer and saw that his gun was gone. I knew what had happened before my brother came to tell me."

"There was no other reason for his taking his gun?" Colonel Primrose asked. "He hadn't been threatened?"

Bartlett Folger glanced at me. "You're referring to

a remark of mine," he said. "That was a mistake on my part. The young man I was talking about has become a very solid citizen. I misjudged him. I'm sorry; I didn't know it at the time."

"I had something else in mind," Colonel Primrose said. "Now that you've brought it up, when did you learn that Bowen Digges was in Mr. Hilyard's office?"

No one looked at Diane. She sat there as calmly as if she'd never heard the name before. I didn't. Sitting as I was on the young man's hat, my position was definitely uncomfortable.

"I can probably answer that better than anyone else," Mrs. Hilyard said. "Mrs. Eaton recognized him at a party and told me. I told my brother on Tuesday, at lunch. I didn't tell Diane, because I didn't want to upset her. She met him accidentally Monday night. I should have told her. All of this might have been avoided."

"Do you mean that if I hadn't met Bowen, father wouldn't have killed himself?" Diane asked. Her voice was small, but distinct and terribly clear.

"If you hadn't kicked up such a———"

"Joan! Stop it!" Mrs. Hilyard turned sharply on her other daughter. "No, Diane. I didn't mean that. But this had been preying on your father's mind for weeks. He didn't want us to come here, in the first place. And I don't think, my dear, you made it any easier for him, if you'll let me say so."

Diane seemed to shrink into a hard, tight little knot.

I could feel her body quivering against mine on the sofa. I took hold of her hand and squeezed it hard between us on the cushion. Her hand was cold as ice, her pulse was pounding.

"I wouldn't be so hard on her, Mrs. Hilyard," Captain Lamb said awkwardly. "She didn't mean——"

Diane flared up like a burning torch. "I did too!" she cried passionately. "I meant to be as cruel to them as they had been to me . . . and Bo, for years and years! I won't be quiet! I don't know why you all want people to think my father killed himself! He didn't! And you all know he didn't! Uncle Bart knew he didn't until he came here and talked to you and Joan and Carey! I was going to say I thought so too. I don't want a scandal any more than the Eatons do, or you do, but I won't say it now! I won't have you all saying I killed my father, because he—he lied to me about Bo. Because it wasn't his fault. He'd never have done it alone! I've never believed it . . . and I don't believe it now!"

She collapsed in a sobbing heap on the sofa, her head in my lap. Mrs. Hilyard sat with her eyes closed, her hands tightly folded, not making a move toward her daughter. How she could have stood it, no matter how "difficult" Diane had ever been, I couldn't see. It was completely heartbreaking.

"I loved him!" she sobbed. "Better than anybody else in the world!"

Everybody sat there as if made of wood, except Colonel Primrose, and he had never been more suave.

"I should like to go back a moment," he said placidly. "I understand that a man has been loitering around the house, Mrs. Hilyard. That was what I had in mind about any threatening——"

"That's absurd, Colonel Primrose," she said calmly. "There has been a beggar around—a crazy old man I gave a dollar to one day. He has kept coming back. You've been listening to the colored servants."

My heart sank. Poor Boston, I thought. I looked at Colonel Primrose. I didn't think he'd let Lilac and me down like this, even if he didn't care about Boston.

"Not at all, Mrs. Hilyard," he said with equal calm. I knew he was saying "Mrs. Latham," actually. "I heard it from a woman across the street. She called headquarters this morning when the radio announced your husband's death. She said a suspicious-looking man had been around for a week or more, watching your house. She thought he might have attacked your husband to rob him when he took the dog out."

"My husband never took the dog out, except Sunday mornings."

"He took him out last night," Colonel Primrose said. "It would seem improbable to me that a man who left his house intending to do away with himself would take his dog along."

Mrs. Hilyard was silent a moment. "The dog may have followed him," she said.

I thought the first sign of doubt had crept into her voice.

Captain Lamb spoke. "Did your husband have any business worries, Mrs. Hilyard?"

"Not in the ordinary sense. The business has been enormously increased. The fact that he was unable to supply the demand for promethium had him almost beside himself. He felt the recent attack on him very keenly. Especially in view of the fact that the new use of promethium in naval communications would probably have saved the life of his son by his first marriage, a month ago. He went down on one of our ships at Pearl Harbor. I think that had more to do with my husband's depression than anything else. All the attacks against him last week about the shortage of promethium added to it—to the point where he was mentally unsound."

There was a silence in the room. Colonel Primrose said, "Did he feel responsible for the present shortage?"

"He did, and without any rational foundation for it. The plant is working twenty-four hours a day. . . . The civilian supply has been completely cut off hasn't it, Bartlett?"

Bartlett Folger nodded. "If we could make promethium out of air, we'd do it gladly, colonel. In our own interest as well as the country's."

Captain Lamb got to his feet. I glanced at Diane. She was watching him, the corners of her red lips drawn down a little, fine crystal tears burning along her lower lashes.

Colonel Primrose got up too. I knew he was watching all of them like an old cat watching half a dozen mice on the pantry shelf.

Mrs. Hilyard rose. "I'm sure, Captain Lamb," she said quietly, "and painful as it is for me to say, that my husband would never have taken his gun and gone out without a hat, in the middle of the night, if he'd been in possession of his normal faculties."

It was as if a bombshell had dropped. I heard Diane's breath break sharply in her throat. Her whole body became as tense and taut as a violin string.

Captain Lamb stopped and looked at her. "Without his . . . hat?" he said blankly.

"His hat is still in the hall closet," Mrs Hilyard said. "He never leaves the house without it, even to go out into the garden."

Captain Lamb's eyes moved slowly past her and rested on Diane. "Where is the hat you said was your father's, Miss Hilyard?" he said.

8

"I'LL HAVE TO HAVE THAT HAT, MISS HILYARD."
It was all illusion, of course, but Captain Lamb seemed
enormous just then, towering grimly above us. Diane
had shrunk deeper into the down cushions, a frail little
orchid of a thing, looking up at him with blank, wide-
eyed innocence. The molehill of the hat had assumed
the proportions of a mountain, and I was sitting on it.

Carey Eaton was completely himself. "She must have
left it out in her car. She didn't have it when she came
in."

Diane turned what Agnes Philips had called "those
incredible hyacinth eyes" on him and said, "Thank you,
dear." As she looked up at Captain Lamb then she was
utterly childlike and disarming.

"I threw it in the canal on the way home. I thought
it was my father's old golf hat until I looked at it again.
Then I realized I'd made a mistake. I threw it out of
the window. Why? Did you want to keep it?"

Captain Lamb controlled himself with an extraordinary effort. "Yes, Miss Hilyard," he said. "Yes. We
did want it. We wanted it very badly. Where did you
throw it over?"

"It must have been at the foot of Foxhall Road,"

she said. "There was a lot of traffic. I suppose it went in. I'm really awfully sorry. Would you like me to go look for it?"

Captain Lamb drew a deep breath. The kind that takes a count of ten before speech can be trusted.

"No, Miss Hilyard," he said heavily. "We'll find it ourselves."

It was fine, of course. At least it would have been if somebody except me had had the hat. Or if I'd been lumpy enough so that a bulge amidships wouldn't be noticeable. But I'm not. I just sat there, wondering whether I could keep on sitting there or if I'd have to get up, and then whether Colonel Primrose would spot it first or that objectionable young man, Mr. Carey Eaton.

Colonel Primrose got up himself. "You'd better get on with it then, Lamb," he said placidly. "It's important to find it. The entire question of suicide or murder hangs on it. If Miss Hilyard believes her father did not take his own life, I'm sure she'll be anxious for us to find it. . . . Do you think you could identify it?"

"I think I could," Diane said helpfully. "Yes, I'm sure I could."

"Did it have initials stamped on it, or the name of the store?" Captain Lamb put in.

"Oh, dear, I didn't notice," Diane said. I thought she was going to turn and say, "Did you, Grace?"

But it was Captain Lamb instead. "Did you, Mrs. Latham?"

I don't like to tell a deliberate lie when Colonel Primrose is looking at me, so I said, "They were very blurred." Which was true enough, and I could have been shaking my head for other reasons.

I drew a long, relieved breath. Colonel Primrose and Captain Lamb started for the door. Carey Eaton and Bartlett Folger followed them out into the hall.

"May I see Mr. Hilyard's hat?" I heard Colonel Primrose ask. "In the hall closet, I think Mrs. Hilyard said."

"Of course," Bartlett Folger said. I saw Mrs. Hilyard give a quick start, and I remembered the broken chair.

"I'll take this along if you don't mind," Colonel Primrose said. "That's a beautiful chair, by the way. I hope you'll get a good man to mend it. I know of one if you'd like his name."

Mrs. Hilyard relaxed and closed her eyes a moment. Her daughter Joan had two bright red spots in her cheeks. I've seldom seen four more relieved women than we were just then, each pair of us for a different reason. But it didn't last long.

Colonel Primrose came back to the door. "Buck's here with your car, Mrs. Latham."

Mrs. Hilyard got up quickly. "My dear, it's been so kind of you to come," she said, holding out her hand.

I could feel Diane's dilemma, being so acutely conscious of my own. She leaned forward. "Mother I'd like Grace to——"

Colonel Primrose interrupted. "You have a luncheon

engagement, Mrs. Latham," he said pleasantly. "It's getting on, and I'd like you to drop me at my house, if you will."

There wasn't much I could do at that point without making a scene, so I got up and said good-by to Diane and Mrs. Hilyard. I didn't look at Diane. I didn't have to. I just stuck my hands in my pockets and followed Colonel Primrose out.

I got to the door of my car. "You'll have to go with Captain Lamb, colonel," I said. "I'm going the other way. I've got to go out to Cabin John." It was the only place I could think of in the opposite direction just then. I got in the car and closed the door.

"No," he said calmly. "You're coming with me. Have you forgotten you're on this case officially?"

"Officially?"

He smiled faintly and nodded. "This time, Mrs. Latham, you're working with the police, and not against them," he said placidly. "You've never been in jail, have you?"

"No," I said.

"All right then. Suppose you drive me back to your house."

He went around the car. I hastily jammed my fur-lined driving gloves into my pocket on top of the rolled-up hat, took an old pair out of the compartment and put them on.

"For your information, Mrs. Latham," he said, getting in beside me, "we're stopping at two places on the way. First at Stanley Woland's, on Adams Place, and second at Bowen Digges'. It may interest you to know Mr. Digges hasn't been at his desk at OPM since Monday afternoon. And that Stanley Woland has been suddenly called out of town."

"Really?" I said. "Stanley was at the ball with Diane last night. His picture was in the paper this morning." I looked at him quickly.

He nodded. "The whole thing, if you'll allow me to say so stinks to heaven. There are a number of things I want to know. One is: Whose hat is Diane hiding? Another is: Who broke the chair in the hall closet? It was leaning against Bartlett Folger's overcoat, so it had obviously been put there since he came in this morning. I want to know why Folger changed his mind and agrees that Hilyard committed suicide when he was tooth and nail against it this morning at eight-fifteen o'clock. Also why Hilyard took his gun when he went out, and why he didn't take his hat. I'd also like to know where all these people were last night."

"Why don't you ask them?"

"Because I'd prefer to ask them each separately."

I turned the car into Adams Place, which is a one-block street running from 33rd to 34th between Q Street and Dent Place. It's a charming little street with old-fashioned lights still on it, where the small two-story, red brick houses once occupied by colored people have been converted into two and three-room maisonettes with tiny walled gardens in back.

Stanley Woland, I knew, was living in one borrowed from a newspaper correspondent who'd gone to China for a couple of months. It was halfway down the block under a gaunt gnarled old oak. As we came up, the curtains in the kitchen window beside the door moved a little and were still again.

"I'll wait," I said. I could at least get Bowen Digges' hat stowed under the seat while the colonel's back was turned.

He shook his head. "I wouldn't want to have to walk home, Mrs. Latham, and I don't trust you. Come along."

It was a long time before I heard steps on the other side of the door. Stanley's Filipino servant opened it just enough to show his face.

"Mr. Woland gone away. Not home today," he said. He started to shut the door promptly, but Colonel Primrose had established a bridgehead with the toe of his shoe. He took a card out of his case and handed it through the crack. The little Filipino looked at it and opened the door hurriedly.

"Mr. Woland very sick," he said earnestly. "He not see people today. You come tomorrow, please?"

"No," Colonel Primrose said calmly. "I'll see him now. Give him that card. We'll wait."

We went through into a rather large room with French doors opening onto the garden. The morning papers were littered about, a cigarette was smoldering where it had been hastily thrown onto the hearth. A half-eaten lunch was on a table. Stanley had left quickly.

He appeared the same way, in pajamas and a Paisley

silk dressing gown, over the banister of the stairs.

"I feel like the devil, colonel," he said apologetically.

He certainly looked it. I stared at him. He had a poultice of some foul greenish stuff over his left eye, and the swollen flesh above and below it was about the same color, perhaps with a little more yellow and purple in it. His other eye was visible through about half its normal channel.

He came on down, not bouncing and bounding now. He stepped very carefully, as if the floor was covered with soap bubbles that he was anxious not to break.

"I had too much champagne last night and a door got in my way," he said. It was a pretty sour attempt to be offhand about it. "Awkward, too, because Mrs. Hilyard called up. It's a ghastly business, isn't it? I should have been over there this morning, but I can't go looking as if I'd been in a tavern brawl. Have you seen Diane, Grace?"

I nodded.

"How is she taking it? She was amazingly fond of the old . . . man."

"After all, he was her father," I observed. "She's taking it very well, on the whole."

Stanley sat down gingerly, Colonel Primrose watching him with considerable interest, though I don't think Stanley knew it.

"I don't know what the devil I'm going to do," Stanley said. "When's the funeral, do you know? Are they going to take him back home?"

"The body has not been released yet," Colonel Primrose said.

Stanley must have jumped inches. "Oh, mother of——" He held on to his head. "What do you mean, released the body?"

His face really was the color of surrealist pork. The perspiration stood out in beads from his poultice to the somewhat receded roots of his hair.

"Is there some question about it? Mrs. Hilyard told me—— Look. Do you mind if I have a drink?"

"Not at all," Colonel Primrose said.

He certainly needed one. The liquor slopped out of the glass and the glass rattled against his teeth. He spilled most of the water he took as a chaser.

"When did you see Mr. Hilyard last, Woland?" Colonel Primrose asked, very affably.

"I don't remember. Let me see. It was——" Stanley looked at Colonel Primrose intently for an instant —or as intently as his condition allowed. "Oh, I might as well be frank."

The telephone rang. Stanley said, "Excuse me, please," started to reach for it, remembered he was out of town, and started to call for his man.

"I'll answer it," Colonel Primrose said. He took it up.

"Hello," he said. . . . "No, this is Colonel Primrose. Do you wish to speak to Mr. Woland?"

He waited a moment and put the phone down. "She hung up," he said calmly.

Stanley moistened his lips. They were swollen, too, and dry gray.

"You were going to be frank, I believe, Woland?"

I thought Stanley gave the impression of a man who couldn't swim about to plunge into an icy stream.

"I saw Hilyard last night when I brought Diane home from the ball," he said. "It was half past ten. We got there at ten. She got a headache, and I thought she ought to go home. She went straight upstairs. Her father came out of the library and asked me to have a nightcap with him."

"He was the door that gave you the black eye?"

"No, he was not!" Stanley said with some irritation. "He wanted to talk to me about Diane. She has done me the honor of consenting to be my wife. Or maybe you've heard?"

I thought Colonel Primrose's failure to extend congratulations was marked.

"I heard it rumored," he said dryly. "It's settled, is it?"

"Yes, it's settled."

"Her father was agreeable?"

"Certainly." Stanley even managed a kind of smile. "With my usual modesty, I can even say he was delighted."

"Well, where did you get the shiner, then?" Colonel Primrose asked.

"I told you once."

"I heard you," Colonel Primrose said. "My patience is infinite, Woland, but I haven't a lot of time."

Stanley looked at him for an instant. "All right. I'll tell you. There was another party present. He and I had a little argument. That's all."

Colonel Primrose nodded. "What's his name?"

"You can find that out for yourself," Stanley said coolly. "I'm not saying."

Colonel Primrose got up. "An icebag would probably help. I hope we haven't disturbed you too much."

I thought Stanley started to give us a distinctly malevolent glance and changed his mind.

"I'll appreciate it if you'll both keep quiet about this . . . eye of mine," he said. "I don't want it all over town."

He gave us, instead, what I suppose was meant to be an ingratiating smile. Actually it was the most horrible, decadent-hued leer you could imagine.

9

"WELL, WELL," COLONEL PRIMROSE SAID, AS WE got back into the car. "I don't know why it always seems funny when somebody hangs one on somebody like Mr. Woland. It isn't, really."

"I know," I answered. "Nevertheless——"

"You and Buck," he remarked. "You're just alike. Romantic and uncivilized, both of you."

I changed the subject. "Who did it?"

"What's your guess?"

"Mr. Carey Eaton," I said. "What's yours?"

He shrugged. "I can't afford to guess, Mrs. Latham. It was Mrs. Hilyard at the phone, by the way. He's probably calling her back now..She——"

When he stopped I said, "Look, colonel. You don't really think she——"

"Shot her husband?" he finished for me.

"Something of the sort."

"I wouldn't say at this point. Somebody did. I think she knows it. She was deliberately lying about that beggar."

"And the hat?" I asked.

He didn't answer for a moment. "I don't know about it. The hat was a mistake. I think she genuinely wanted us to believe it was suicide."

"Why?"

He smiled. "Didn't your mother teach you it was un-attractive for women to ask a man questions he can't answer? Bowen Digges lives with three other bachelors in a tenant house on the Folsom place across the river. Do you know where it is?"

"I know where the Folsom place is," I said.

"Will you take me there, please?"

"I thought I had a luncheon engagement," I answered. "I'm going to be awfully late to it. What's the matter with your car?"

"It's not mine, it's Buck's," he said imperturbably. "He's using it. He's taken that cigarette pack and Lawrason Hilyard's hat down to the laboratory at head-quarters. If he had the hat that Lamb's dragging the canal for, he could have taken that too."

"Whose do you think it was?" I asked, as calmly as I could.

"It was a young man's. Not Woland's, unless he changed before he took Diane home. It could be Eaton's. It could belong to a man named Duncan Scott —a young lawyer Hilyard had an appointment with last night."

"How do you know that?"

"Scott told me so yesterday afternoon. He has two clients he's trying to get priority ratings for. He came down for one and picked up the other—a fellow named Ira Colton—down here. He and Colton met Digges at a party. Digges agreed to lunch with them yesterday and talk it over, but he didn't show up. They ran into Hilyard as they were leaving. He said they could come and see him at his house at nine o'clock."

I remembered something. "Mr. Colton's the gadget manufacturer from somewhere near Cleveland, isn't he?" I asked. "Bowen Digges was talking about him Monday afternoon. They must have got together after I left. I suppose that's why he was invited. Digges, I mean."

We'd come to the Key Bridge. I could see a couple of policemen in a boat, rowing slowly down the canal, poking around among the water hyacinths and irises along the bank. I felt my cheeks getting unnaturally warm. It occurred to me that he hadn't mentioned Bowen Digges as a possible owner of the hat, which could mean a lot.

"Bowen Digges said Colton had been practically ruined by not being able to get promethium," I said hastily.

"So Duncan Scott told me. Now, if Colton had committed suicide, I could understand it. He's on the spot, like a great many other small manufacturers of luxury items."

"Do you think Mr. Hilyard was really responsible for the shortage?"

Colonel Primrose didn't answer for a moment. "He's

got the blame for it, from people who don't know the facts," he answered then. "What his wife said about it is probably true, up to the point of his killing himself. What Folger said is right. There's been no hoarding, and no bootlegging to favored customers. I went into that a month ago. There was a rumor they were holding out."

We'd crossed the bridge to the Virginia side. I turned right past the brewery, up the Potomac.

"I ran that rumor down a couple of weeks ago," he went on. "Or I think I did. It came originally from this Colton. He wouldn't say where he'd picked it up, at any rate—if anywhere. I suppose it cropped up when the FBI found carloads of critical material that foreign agents had bought up, lying around in freight yards and warehouses. On the theory that if they couldn't use them, it would be a good idea to keep us from using them. No promethium was found. The FBI, the Bureau of Internal Revenue and the Interstate Commerce Commission all checked it, and I took a hand for Army and Navy Intelligence. I can say with authority there's nothing in it."

The big Folsom place on the river had been closed a long time. I'd heard that a couple of years ago they fixed up the tenant house, a hundred yards or so from the road off the main highway, and let groups of young men connected with the Government have it rent free, just to have some responsible people on the place. Mr. Bowen Digges was apparently one of the present lot.

When we got there, a cleaner's van was just stopping in front of the house, and a colored maid had just come out on the porch. We got out.

"Is Mr. Digges in?" Colonel Primrose asked.

"Yes, sir, but he's asleep," the maid said. "They said nobody was to wake him. The phone's been ringing all morning. I ain't going to wake him for nobody."

"We'd like to wait, in that case," Colonel Primrose said.

"Yes, sir."

She went into the living room ahead of us, put the windows down and lighted the fire. I glanced around. It was an impersonal room, sparsely furnished, but fresh and clean. There were a lot of pipes in a rack on the mantel, and some enormous ash trays sitting about. Several suits waiting for the cleaner, I supposed, were lying across the arm of a sofa in front of the window.

Colonel Primrose went over and sat down by them.

"Goodness me," he said.

The surprised tone of his voice was about the falsest sound I'd ever heard. My heart sank. He'd picked up a pair of gray flannel trousers, and was examining the legs with as completely phony disinterest as I've ever seen him guilty of.

The maid looked up from the fire. She smiled. "I don't know if they're ever going to look right again. Mr. Digges just bought them last week."

Colonel Primrose picked up the matching coat and vest.

"Did Mr. Digges tell you to send these to the cleaner?"

"No, sir. Some things I don't need to be told."

Colonel Primrose put them down by him. "I'm afraid I'll have to keep them for a while," he said calmly. He took out his card case again. "Give this to Mr. Digges. Tell him I have to see him at once."

The colored woman's face changed almost ludicrously. She stood there stupidly for a moment, took the card and went silently out.

"That was rather . . . abrupt, wasn't it?" I asked.

"Come have a look."

He picked up one trouser leg and held it toward me. One look was enough, and I didn't even have to take a step toward him. The brown stains were horribly visible from where I was. The cuffs had been wet and were stiff and splotched with mud.

"The trouble with you," Colonel Primrose said, "is that you're still letting your sympathies make hash of your thinking. You like Diane; Diane's in love with Digges; Digges had nothing to do with the death of Lawrason Hilyard. It doesn't matter at all how much blood there is on his trouser leg."

I didn't say anything. Put that way, my position was not highly tenable.

"If I'd known we were going to have a murder on our hands, I'd never have mentioned Hilyard to you," he went on. "I don't want to have you—once more—concealing evidence, let's say, because nice people are involved. A lot of nice people have been hanged, my dear, and a lot more would have been if there weren't people like you and Buck and Lamb who don't think nice people can do not-nice nice things."

He came over to my chair. I hadn't realized how guilty, or something, the expression on my face must have been.

"Don't look like that," he said gently. "I'm sorry. I didn't mean to hurt your feelings. Go on being an obstructionist. I like it, really, or I'd have had you in jail years ago." Then, surprisingly, he raised my hand and kissed it.

"You've been seeing too much of Stanley Woland, Colonel Primrose," I said.

He chuckled. "There you go again. You'd just as soon hang that poor devil. He wouldn't kill a fly. All he's trying to do is get a maximum out of life with a minimum of work. Just put him out of that charming head of yours, Mrs. Latham."

I didn't have time to protest. There was the sound of heavy feet on the flimsy stairs. Colonel Primrose went back to the sofa just as Bowen Digges came in. He was in his shirt sleeves, with his collar open and no tie.

"Oh, I'm sorry," he said. "I didn't know there was a la—— Oh, how do you do, Mrs. Latham."

"This is Colonel Primrose, Mr. Digges," I said.

He strode across the room and held out his hand. "Glad you're around, sir. I've heard a lot about you. You were investigating promethium, I understand."

Colonel Primrose's manner was affable, for all his warning about the smiler with the knife under the cloak and the trousers with the blood on the leg. However, I knew he always was. Bowen Digges was not affable, exactly. He looked like a man who'd just stuck his head under the cold-water faucet, and I expect that's exactly what he'd done. His thick crisp thatch was still wet, his face rosy, if unshaven. All the humor and good nature I'd thought so attractive Monday afternoon were gone. He looked haggard and not very happy. After the lecture I'd just got I knew I shouldn't let myself feel sorry for him. But I did anyway.

"I'm investigating something else just now," Colonel Primrose said.

"Do you mind if I get a cup of coffee, and I'll be right with you?" His eyes fell then on the gray flannel suit. "I'm sorry. Let me get this thing out of sight."

"That's what I'm investigating, I'm afraid," Colonel Primrose said.

Bowen Digges' face changed. "Oh," he said. "In that case, I'd better leave it, no doubt. Do you mind if I get the coffee just the same?"

"Not at all."

Just then the maid appeared at the back door with a tray, and put it down by him.

"Thanks," he said. . . . "Would you like some, Mrs. Latham?"

I shook my head. He turned to Colonel Primrose.

"All right. Shoot."

My blood ran a little cold. It was the old association-of-words tests they used to give you in Psychology I.

10

"I UNDERSTAND YOU WEREN'T AT YOUR OFFICE at all yesterday, Mr. Digges?"

"That's right. I'm not there today, and I don't expect to be there tomorrow, or any time in the future, if you're interested."

"Why not?"

"That's my business, if you don't mind, colonel. And so far as I know, it has nothing to do with that state of my pants."

"I'd like to be sure of it," Colonel Primrose said equably. "When did you see Lawrason Hilyard last?"

"Last night." Bowen Digges put down his cup. His gray eyes had a tinge of brimstone in them, and so did his voice. "Why?"

"I was wondering. At what time, do you recall?"

"Of course. From nine-thirty on."

"Until when?"

"Around midnight. I don't remember the minute. Again why?"

The telephone jangled noisily out in the hall.

"Excuse me," Bowen Digges said. He came back in a minute and sat down on the sofa again.

"All right, colonel. Go ahead," he said. His face hadn't changed, but he seemed harder and tighter than he'd been before.

Colonel Primrose looked at him for some time. "Are you still leaving?" he asked quietly.

A sardonic flicker lighted the young man's eyes. He put his hand in his pocket and fished out a crumpled pack of cigarettes. It looked empty to me, but there was still one in it. When he had taken it out he twisted the pack and tossed it into the wastebasket.

"Not right away, colonel," he said.

It doesn't prove a thing, I told myself. *Lots of people do that.*

Colonel Primrose's face was as placid as Buddha's. It was Bowen who broke the silence. "I hear it was suicide. I take it you don't think so?"

"I'll have to be convinced, Digges."

Bowen nodded. "So will I." He looked down at the pile of gray flannel on the sofa between them. "I'm the Number One Boy, then. Is that it?"

He was so cool about it that I thought even Colonel Primrose was a little annoyed.

"Did you wear a hat last night, by any chance?" he inquired.

Bowen Digges looked puzzled. "I believe I did," he said, after an instant. "Yes, I know I did. I thought I'd better dress up to go to the boss' house. I went by invitation—to see a lawyer and his client who wants promethium."

"You had a luncheon engagement with them yesterday?"

"Yes. It slipped my mind. I'd already told them there wasn't a chance. A free lunch wouldn't have changed anything."

"What happened?"

"Last night? Nothing. I just told them again."

"They were annoyed, I suppose?" Colonel Primrose said.

"I think you could say so. I don't suppose anybody threatens to put you in the pen if they're pleased about things."

"You, or Hilyard?"

"Both of us. Hilyard first, of course. Me as an accessory, or cat's-paw, or something."

"Where is your hat now, by the way?" Colonel Primrose asked.

Bowen looked a little blank. "Upstairs, I guess. Or out in the car. I don't wear one much, so I don't keep track of it. Once more, why?"

"Were you on the towing path of the Georgetown Canal last night?"

"Yes. I took Mr. Hilyard down to M Street in my car, and walked along the path with him to give his dog a run. He said he wanted to talk to me. We walked about a mile, I guess, and came back."

Colonel Primrose hesitated an instant. "Did he have his hat?"

Bowen Digges stared at him for a while.

"Why——" he began, and stopped. "Of course," he said. "He got his hat out of the closet when we left, and handed me mine."

"You took him back home, then, when you'd finished your walk?" Colonel Primrose suggested. There was no change in his face or voice.

"No. I left him down on the path calling his dog. Just at the end of the little bridge."

"You came straight home then?"

"After a while."

"What time?"

"I don't know exactly."

"When did you leave Hilyard?"

"Midnight, or a little later."

Colonel Primrose looked steadily at him for an instant. "Well," he said, "where did you pick these up?"

He pointed to the brown stains on the trouser leg, on the sofa between them.

"You've got me," Bowen Digges said quietly. "I hadn't noticed them until just now."

"Did you wear an overcoat too?"

Bowen nodded.

"Ask your maid to get it, please."

I was watching Colonel Primrose much more intently than I was Bowen Digges. I had the kind of dread you have in a dream where everything seems outwardly normal and yet you're aware, when you wake, of a terrible anxiety that you can't define. Though this was easily definable, outwardly at least. And when the maid brought down a heavy gray tweed overcoat it was more defined than ever.

"I guess you're still right, colonel," Bowen said quietly.

I've heard people talk about inanimate evidence, but I'd never seen it so clearly as I did then. The dark splotches of blood over the front of the soft tweed hadn't got there passively. They had spurted out onto it. He hadn't brushed against a bleeding wound; he'd been there when the wound was made. And that wasn't the worst of it. The sleeves were stained too.

I looked back at Colonel Primrose. His black eyes were snapping.

"It's time you did a little explaining, Digges," he said curtly.

It seemed to me that it was then for the first time that Bowen Digges realized something was happening. He stood looking down at the horrible mess on his overcoat, his face hardening slowly. Tiny white ridges came out along his jaw. His mouth closed into a thin hard line. And I leaned back in my chair with a kind of sense of relief. He was doing some serious thinking at last, and he'd say something. And he did, but not what I'd hoped he would.

"I see," he said. He met Colonel Primrose's steady gaze with one just as steady. "I'm not doing any explaining. I've told you everything I'm going to. You'll have to take it or leave it."

He was standing there facing Colonel Primrose, his

back to the hall door. I suppose I must have heard a footfall out there, though I wasn't consciously aware of it, even when I turned and looked that way. I jumped in my chair. Diane Hilyard was there. Her hair was blown back from her face, her cheeks red from the cold. But the red was fading from them even then. She was staring across the room past Bowen, her eyes fixed on that suit lying there on the sofa, the bloodstains horribly and cruelly displayed. Her hand moved slowly to the doorframe and clutched it. Her lips parted, she swayed a little and caught herself. Her face was colorless.

"No," Colonel Primrose said curtly. He hadn't seen her; Bowen Digges was in his line of vision. "Not me. The district attorney . . . and twelve men on the jury."

"The district attorney and twelve men on the jury, then," Bowen Digges said. He nodded down at the clothes. "You'll want to take these. I'll get you some paper to wrap them in."

"I'd like to ask you one more question first," Colonel Primrose said, as equably and suavely as ever. "Was there ever any question about Lawrason Hilyard not being right-handed?"

Bowen looked at him for an instant. "I never heard it questioned," he said calmly. "I happen to know he was left-handed. I've known him most of my life. You know that already, I guess."

Colonel Primrose took a step toward him.

"I know," he said very deliberately, "that he paid

you twenty-five hundred dollars to leave town and not
marry his daughter."

I felt rather than heard the gasp that came from the
hall doorway. Diane's hand tightened on the door-
frame. Bowen had started toward a table covered with
newspapers. He stopped dead and turned slowly back.

"Come again, colonel?" he asked very slowly.

His face had gone quite white. I wished to heaven
there was more space between them.

"I said, I knew the Hilyards paid you twenty-five
hundred dollars," Colonel Primrose repeated, "to leave
town and not marry Diane Hilyard."

Bowen stood there looking at him. "That's what I
thought you said, colonel. Would you mind telling me
who told you that?"

The atmosphere in the room was so charged that I
thought everything was going to explode in our faces. I
saw Diane raise her hand to her mouth to stifle a cry,
her eyes wide with alarm. Bowen Digges took a step
forward. He was a hundred and eighty pounds or so of
taut cold steel, his eyes shuttered and dangerous. I held
my breath.

"Is it true, Digges, or isn't it?" Colonel Primrose
said.

The young man's jaw went harder. "I asked who
told you."

"It doesn't matter. It's been told, and it's generally
believed. I'm asking you whether it's a fact."

Bowen Digges relaxed slowly. Diane had let her

hand fall and was waiting, holding her breath, her eyes bright and body tense.

"It is not true," Bowen said steadily. "It's false. The Hilyards all know it."

Colonel Primrose turned a little. "Did you know it, Miss Hilyard?"

I might have known all the time he knew she was there. I certainly ought to know by this time that he doesn't have to look at things to see them.

Digges whirled around and stared at her blankly. The muscles of his face contracted for an instant with something that looked so much like unbearable pain that I winced. Then a slow flush spread from his open collar to the roots of his hair. Diane hadn't taken her eyes off him. Her face was still pale, but two spots of color burned slowly in her cheeks. Her eyes were burning too, like smoldering blue coals. She let go the door-frame and stood there erect, her chin up.

"I know it is true," she said. "I've seen the check. I . . . wouldn't have believed it, ever, ever, till my father showed it to me. And that's why he didn't tell . . . anybody you were here. He didn't lie. You wouldn't dare say it if he were . . . still alive."

Bowen Digges' face had gone hard and flat again. "Okay," he said shortly. "If that's what you want to believe, you can." He turned to Colonel Primrose. "If you'll excuse me, I'd like to get dressed."

11

DIANE'S VOICE CAME FROM DOWN IN A
miserable little huddle of brown fur beside me on the
car seat, sounding tragically small and lost: "Why did
I do that?"

I was taking her to town. Colonel Primrose was waiting to take Bowen in to see Captain Lamb, and Diane
had come in a taxi to avoid another scene with her
brother-in-law, Carey Eaton, who'd put her car keys in
his pocket to keep her from leaving the house.

"I really don't know," I said, though it was fairly
obvious. "First you get both of us in a mess trying to
save him, then you confirm the only unattractive thing
anybody has to say about him. Whatever made you
come out, in the first place?"

She didn't say anything for a minute. "I . . . had to
see him, to . . . tell him something," she said uncer-
tainly. "And I wanted to tell him he's got to be careful,
but he—he doesn't have to worry about his hat."

I agreed wryly. "No. It's us that have to worry about
that."

"Where is it now?"

"In my pocket, darling," I said. "Colonel Primrose hasn't let me out of his sight. He's an awful lot smarter than he looks, and it's just as well not to forget it."

"We've got to get rid of it," she answered quickly. "Can't you do it? I don't dare take it home, not with Carey Eaton always snooping around."

I didn't say anything.

After a moment she said, "Grace."

"Yes?"

"Where did all that . . . blood on Bowen's coat come from?"

"Look, Diane," I said, more abruptly than I'd meant to. "I don't know. But I know this—and you ought to face it: Bowen Digges is in a bad spot. Your father's watch stopped at eleven thirty-five. Bowen doesn't know it, and Colonel Primrose didn't tell him. And Bowen said he was with your father, down on the towing path, until midnight or later. That's practically enough to hang him, without anything else at all."

"He didn't do it," she said calmly.

"How do you know he didn't?"

"Because."

So far as I know, there's never since Eve been a better way to end an argument, and perhaps it's just as well. We crossed the bridge to Georgetown in two separate and distinct spheres of silence. I was wondering about Colonel Primrose again, and Diane was doing a little quiet thinking of her own.

"Grace," she said slowly, "maybe—maybe father did

do it, himself. Maybe mother's right. She says nobody can ever prove he didn't.''

I glanced around at her. It was pathetically unconvincing. More than that, it was an unconsciously but definitely alarming picture of her mother. And what happened that night didn't relieve it any.

The evening editions were pretty ghastly. The bodies of thousands of men piled up on the war fronts in a single afternoon were pushed to the inside pages to make space for that single body in the C. & O. Canal. The headlines in themselves were bad enough: POLICE PROBE "SUICIDE OF OPM CHIEF. HINT FOUL PLAY IN CANAL MYSTERY. POLICE SEARCH CANAL FOR MISSING HAT. DEAD DOLLAR-A-YEAR MAN MADE MILLIONS IN NEW METAL. CITIZENS DEMAND POLICE SHAKE-UP. CANAL HAS COLORFUL HISTORY. CLUBWOMAN DEMANDS DRAINING OF CANAL.

The pictures were worse. There was a full page of diagrams of the canal, with Lawrason Hilyard's body drawn in, apparently by the editor's three-year-old child. Pages of all the papers were devoted to pictures of Diane running along the retaining wall and down the stairs, crossing the canal, and standing there for that moment with Sergeant Buck holding her. There was a picture of Sheila bringing me that hat. There were pictures of the Hilyards' house, here and back home; Joan Eaton's picture in her wedding gown, her and Carey's house in Georgetown. There was a picture of Bartlett Folger's yacht, the Samarkand, moored in the Potomac

Basin. All of them were appropriately and sensationally titled. If publicity was what Joan and Carey Eaton had wanted to avoid, I knew there'd be trouble in the house on Prospect Street. And when I saw my own picture there on the canal, with my name as that of an old friend of the family who'd come with Diane on her tragic pilgrimage, I canceled a supper engagement and stayed at home.

It was half past nine, and I was writing a letter to Agnes Philips, back in the Hilyards' home town, when the phone rang. My mind flew instantly to the missing hat, safely parked now in the chest-on-chest in the upstairs hall, under a long damask tablecloth that we use only on Thanksgiving and Christmas. I was still expecting Colonel Primrose to catch up with me momentarily.

It was Diane, however, and she was frightened. I knew that before she said it.

"Grace, can you come over?" Her voice had a definite quality of fear. "I'm so scared. I'm all alone. I hate to ask you. The servants were afraid to stay, so mother let them go home to sleep. She's out, too, and the house is so—so quiet."

I'm not very brave myself. It's only when someone else is hysterically less so that I can put on a kind of front and believe in it for a few minutes. But I went. Diane was waiting at the sitting-room window where I'd sat with her mother the day I called. The street had never seemed so forlorn or deserted before, or so full of deep shadowy places where things could lurk and creep silently out. It was getting a little warmer. A soft misty fog was beginning to settle down, giving everything a vague, luminous sort of Whistler quality, so that nothing seemed very real or solid.

Diane opened the door with a little half sob of relief. Her hands were cold and she was trembling fitfully.

"I'm just a coward," she said. "I never knew I was before. I guess I've never been alone in a house in all my life. It's all so—so————" She shivered convulsively. "I keep hearing things."

"I know," I said. "Where's your mother?"

"She went over to the Eatons'. I didn't go. Did you see the papers?"

I nodded.

"Joan and Carey are in a state. I shouldn't have gone down there, I guess. Come on in the library; there's a fire. . . . Come on, boy."

It was the first time I'd seen their spaniel. He was frightened, too—staying as close to her heels as he could get, his long ears drooping, as scared as if he expected a savage rabbit to leap out of a corner at him. He settled down at her feet in front of the fire, trembling all over his silky little body.

"He makes me more frightened than I really am," Diane said. "He keeps going upstairs to father's door and crying as if he thought he'd come back. This afternoon he started howling. That's when Boston and Annie got frightened and wouldn't stay after dark."

The spaniel whined. A dry branch scraped against the window and a shutter rattled somewhere. There wasn't a radio in the room, and if there had been we'd probably have tuned in exactly on the latest police report about Lawrason Hilyard's death.

"When did you first know Bowen, Diane?" I asked. Maybe it wasn't too tactful, but I thought if I could get her mind on the distant past it would help a little.

She stared into the fire. "Since I was a kid. He delivered papers. That was before his father died. Bo was in high school. His father was a technician in the plant. They got some kind of employees' compensation. That's when his mother bought the little store. She'd been a schoolteacher, but she wasn't well enough to go with that, and the children could do lots of things to help. She even took care of the gas and oil when the children were at school. I thought she had a lot of—of courage."

The spaniel woke up with a start, growling. The hair on his back stood up. He barked sharply.

"Hush," Diane said.

She had straightened up herself and was listening, and so was I. From somewhere there came the low grating sound of a rusty hinge. The dog stiffened, growled again, ran to the back windows and began pawing at the heavy drawn curtains.

Diane got up slowly. "Somebody must be out in the garden," she whispered. "Here, Peter. Lie down."

The dog was shaking again, sensing the sudden alarm in her voice.

I reached for the telephone. "I'm going to call the police," I said, being practical for once in my life.

She shook her head quickly. "No, I'd rather not. I

wanted to ask them tonight to—to sort of stay around, but mother wouldn't let me. She doesn't want any more publicity than we've had."

I got up, went over to the window, drew the curtain back, stepped inside it and pulled it behind me so the light wouldn't shine out. Down below, the lights from the bridge twinkled through the long shroud of fog along the line of the river. The garden was on the level of the basement rooms, and sloped down in broad planes about half a block to the retaining wall above M Street. It looked like a ghost garden in the vague luminous mist. The snow had melted or been swept from the brick wall. Three wooden chairs stood out ghastly white through the bare leprous-spotted branches of the big sycamore tree on the second terrace. I looked at the wooden gate in the ivy-covered wall along 37th Street. It was closed, and the whole garden was as silent and motionless as a graveyard.

Then suddenly my heart was in my throat and my spine was crawling, cold as ice. A tall black-shrouded figure appeared out of the shadow of a great burlap-covered box bush and moved slowly, as slowly as a sleep-walker, across the terrace to the chairs under the silver-splotched tree, and returned as slowly, stopping every few feet to look back at the gate in the wall, and then move on again.

Diane grasped at my arm. I hadn't realized she'd moved in with me behind the curtain. Her breath made a sharp sibilant sound in her throat.

"It's mother!" she whispered.

Neither of us moved. Mrs. Hilyard reached the end of the terrace and came back again. I could see her face for an instant, gleaming white under the black shawl she wore around her head. I couldn't see it plainly, but it gave an impression of age, and of something else I couldn't define, and still can't.

She went back along the terrace, stopped and looked at the wooden gate again. She raised her left hand, pushed up her sleeve and held her hand up as if trying to see the time in the frail light through the hazy mist. Then she sat down slowly, a terrible figure, black against the gleaming whiteness of the garden chair. It made the two others emptier and hideously gaunt. She was like one of the Weird Sisters waiting for the two others at the rendezvous on the blasted heath.

I don't know how long she sat there. It seemed very long to me, and must have seemed longer to Diane. "What do you suppose——" she whispered.

I shook my head.

The dog growled again. I heard that same grating of a rusty hinge. The garden gate opened slowly, and closed. Out of the shadow a man came. He was tall and thin and wasted. He stood for a moment looking around him. Mrs. Hilyard got up slowly. The man saw her, and came to meet her by the terrace steps. He took off his hat. She motioned with her hand toward the chairs.

As he turned his head the light caught his face for just an instant. It was the man who'd stood across the street, the man she'd said was a beggar. He was the man the police were searching all Washington to find—who had talked about the devil until Boston was afraid to take the dog out for a walk after night had fallen.

12

DIANE AND I MOVED AWAY FROM THE
window and let the heavy cherry-red curtain slip back
into place. Neither of us spoke. She went slowly across
the room to the sofa and sat down, staring ahead of her
into nothing, her face white. The dog watched her
anxiously, made that soft little sound that spaniels do,
and touched her knee with his paw. She put her hand
down automatically and rubbed his ears.

The silence crept out of the corners and lay like a pall
over the house. A log burned through in the middle
slipped down from the andirons. I jumped as if a tree
had fallen there. The spaniel raised his head, growling
softly.

Diane looked at me and looked away again.

"I think I'd better go," I said. I started to get up.

"No, please!" she said quickly. "Wait. I—I
couldn't—"

She didn't finish it, but I knew what she meant. She
was afraid to be there alone when her mother came in.
It seemed a terrible thing, but I, for one, certainly
didn't blame her. I was waiting there, too, for the door

to open and Mrs. Hilyard to come in, with a kind of cold dread paralyzing my will to talk and to seem casual and natural when she did come.

The spaniel made a rush for the door, suddenly, barking. I heard a key turn in the lock and the door open.

"Hello, Peter. Down, Peter. Don't jump." Mrs. Hilyard's voice was short, and it sounded tired—or weary rather than tired, weary and strained.

"Diane?" she called, as if she weren't sure the girl would be there.

Diane took a deep breath and closed her eyes for a second. "Yes, mother," she said. It was spoken so naturally I could hardly believe it was the same girl. Then, as if preparing her, she added, "Grace is here, mother."

There was a short silence. Then Mrs. Hilyard came across the hall to the library door. It was a little startling, seeing her there—not because she looked startling, but because she didn't. Her long black covered-up dinner dress, the black Persian-lamb coat draped around her shoulders, the black lace scarf she carried in her hand had none of the sinister robed quality they'd had when she was pacing so slowly along the terrace. She looked as any bereaved woman would look, coming in from dining quietly with her married daughter, stopping in to speak before she went up to her room. Her face was very pale, with tired lines around the mouth and eyes, which was natural enough. There were only two things that weren't right. One was the red lipstick, freshly and hastily put on with a not very steady hand.

The other was a kind of inner conflict that seemed to go beyond the plain ordinary irritation that showed as she came into the room and that all her casualness couldn't quite conceal.

"I'm so glad you came," she said. The muscles of her face moved in the orthodox pattern of a social smile. "I was worried about Diane being here by herself. Did you just decide to come?"

"I called her up and asked her," Diane answered for me. "And I did call Stanley. You see, I am an obedient child. He thinks it's mumps he's got. The doctor's got him incommunicado."

"I didn't insist on your calling him," her mother said a little curtly. "I thought it would be a nice thing for you to do, when he's been so thoughtful."

Diane, it was plain, didn't know what had happened to her one-time count. I couldn't tell whether Mrs. Hilyard did or not, though I rather doubted it. It struck me, too, that this was the first time Diane had mentioned him all day. He certainly didn't seem to occupy much of her mind.

I realized just then that Mrs. Hilyard was looking across Diane's head at the window. Her hand moved quickly as she steadied herself against the edge of the table by her.

"What have you two been doing?" she asked pleasantly.

"Just talking," Diane said. "How are Mr. and Mrs. Eaton?"

Mrs. Hilyard flared up like a piece of oiled paper with a match touched to it. "Diane! I've asked you a hundred times to stop calling them that, and I want you to do it! You act as if they were no relation to you whatever! And get that dog off the sofa! I'm sick and tired of——"

She stopped abruptly, gripping the side of the table. Her hand in the half circle of light under the green shade impressed me again as it had that first day. It was almost shockingly determined. She dropped it to her side again and took a deep breath. Diane was looking at her calmly and without surprise.

"I beg your pardon, both of you," Mrs. Hilyard said unsteadily. "I'm . . . nervous and upset. I think I'd better go upstairs. . . . You'll excuse me, please, Mrs. Latham."

"I didn't mean to irritate you, mother," Diane said. "I just call them that for fun. . . . You get down, Peter."

She gave the dog a little push off the sofa.

"Well, stop it, please," her mother said shortly. . . . "Good night, Mrs. Latham."

I heard her heels clicking sharply on the stairs, and her door close. Peter, the dog, jumped up on the sofa again and settled down.

Diane stood up suddenly and stood there looking down at a small wadded piece of paper lying on the floor by the table where her mother had been standing. She must have had it in her hand and dropped it when she became aware of the window so abruptly. Diane went over and picked it up. I watched her unravel it. She looked at it for a minute and handed it to me.

It was a cheaply printed leaflet, of the sort that are sometimes left in mailboxes by wandering sectarians who believe the Day of Judgment is at hand. This one was on that subject, with verses from the Old Testament and Revelation to prove it. "Who is that man, Diane?" I asked.

She went to the door, listened for a moment and came back. "Mother said we weren't to talk about him," she said slowly. "I don't know why. He never tried to talk to me. Once he handed me one of those things, about the wicked flourishing like a green bay tree or something. I suppose he's sort of cracked. I came in one night, and mother and father were having an awful row about him. I didn't ask anything and they didn't tell me."

She stood there looking down into the fire. I got up and put my coat on. She watched me unhappily.

"I hate to leave you," I said.

"Not so much as I hate being left." She smiled suddenly. "I'll be all right. I just wish I didn't have to go to bed. Maybe I won't."

"You go to bed, and go to sleep," I said.

She picked the spaniel up and carried him in her arms to the door with me. I waved back at them as I started down the street. They looked almost unbearably alone and pathetic, standing there under the fanlight in that silent shadowy street. If thcy'd really been alone I don't think I should have been as unhappy about leaving them there.

It took me hours to get to sleep. Every time I dropped off I waked with a start. A tall black figure kept walking slowly across some kind of ghostly corridor of my dreams. I could open my eyes and still see those three white chairs, empty and motionless, in a bleak and distorted garden that was half my own and half a terrifying wasteland with water all around it.

Suddenly I woke again, the telephone buzzing in my ear. I reached for it quickly.

"Grace, it's Diane. She's gone out again—mother, I mean. I heard her go down the stairs and close the front door. She changed her dress, but she hasn't been in bed at all. What can I do?"

Her voice was so sharp with alarm, and I was in such a state myself that I'd have completely misunderstood her if she hadn't gone on. "Grace! What if something happens to her?"

That had me stopped, frankly. The idea that Mrs. Hilyard might be a victim instead of an active agent hadn't occurred to me. Nor had I thought Diane had the kind of faith in her mother that made her blind to all the implications of the scene on the terrace. But apparently she did, and it wasn't my business to try to disillusion her. So, instead of saying, "I think your mother can look after herself very well, my dear," I said, "I'd go back to bed, if I were you, and try to go to sleep again. She must know what she's doing. Or come over and stay with me."

I could almost see her shaking her head.

"I can't leave her here alone," she said. "She'd be upset. I'll just wait."

"If she doesn't come back pretty soon, call me and we'll do something," I said.

I looked at the clock. It was quarter to two. And it was eight o'clock when I woke up again. Lilac was putting the papers on my bed. She went over to put down the windows.

Among her other functions, Lilac acts as a spiritual rheumatic joint. I can tell what the weather's going to be in our household for the next day by those first few minutes in the morning. Cloudy, with the glass falling rapidly, was the barometric reading now, as she went out, got my tray and put it across my lap without so much as a moody mutter.

"That chair," she said then, abruptly.

"What chair?"

"That chair she's tryin' to make pretense came apart when somebody set on it. Boston, he say that man broke it. He come out of there blood-mad, Boston say. Shoutin' he come after some kind of pie, and ain' nobody goin' to keep him from gettin' it."

"What man, Lilac?" I asked patiently. I've never known whether she thinks I really know about all the people and things she's talking about and am just trying to make pretense I'm being obtuse.

"The one that came first," she said. "He come with another man, tryin' to make pretense he's a lawyer. Who ever heard of a lawyer goin' roun' people's houses bus'in' up the furniture? Wantin' some kind of pie."

I understood, vaguely. "Pierorities, maybe?" I said.

"Tha's it. I ain' never heard talk of it till jus' recently."

There didn't seem to be any point trying to explain, so I let it go. I was much more interested in the headlines screaming up at me from the front pages anyway.

DEAD OPM CHIEF HAD RESIGNED, I read.

"That man come out in th' hall blood-mad," Lilac said. "The one that called hisself a lawyer tryin' to hang on to his coattails. But he go back an' slam the door shut, an' that's when the chair got smashed. Boston, he peekin' 'round the staircase, don' know what goin' to happen next. People comin' in an' goin' out, rarin' around sayin' they is an' they ain'. Boston says he ain' never worked for them kind of people in his life."

"Well, I wouldn't talk about it," I said.

"Ah ain' goin' to talk 'bout it. Ah don' want nothin' to do with them kind of people."

I poured a cup of coffee and picked up the paper:

It was revealed late last night that Lawrason Hilyard, whose body was found in the Chesapeake and Ohio Canal yesterday morning, had sent his resignation to the Office of Production Management. It was postmarked 10:30 and sent from a Georgetown branch of the post office. At OPM it was said that Mr. Hilyard's reasons given were ill health and the pressure of private business. No further details were made public. It is believed, however, that the police regard the resignation as evidence to support the theory of suicide held by the family. When questioned about it at the home of Mr. and Mrs. Carey Eaton last night, Mrs. Hilyard refused to comment, except to say she had known for some time that her husband had intended to resign his OPM position. She did not know he had actually done so. He had no enemies, Mrs. Hilyard said. Her son-in-law, Carey Eaton, confirmed her statements. The family would leave Washington as soon as the necessary arrangements were made, he said.

The next column was headed, SEARCH FOR MYSTERY MAN CONTINUES. It said:

The police revealed late last night that the search for a man known to have been seen near the dead OPM branch chief's mansion on Prospect Street was still being prosecuted. As descriptions of the man given by neighbors and by the servants in the Hilyard household vary considerably, the police are understood to be working out a composite picture similar to that constructed in the Bruno Hauptmann case, which will be issued shortly. It is believed the man may have followed the metal magnate when he left his Prospect Street residence to take his dog for a walk. He was last seen stand-

ing at the end of the Georgetown University campus
wall across the street from the Hilyard house at about
eight o'clock last night. He was found——

It went on with a rehash of yesterday's details.

A bulletin in heavier type in the middle of the page
caught my eye. It was headed POLICE QUESTION UN-
IDENTIFIED MAN. My heart chilled as I read it.

A man whose name was not revealed and whose
identity the police are shielding for the present is known
to have appeared at headquarters yesterday afternoon.
(Continued on page thirteen.)

I turned the pages quickly.

It was learned that he had gone through a police
line-up and had been identified by Joseph Bascombe,
a waterman, as the person he had seen· running along
the towing path a little before midnight Tuesday. Mr.
Hilyard, it has been authoritatively stated, died at about
11:35 that night. The police are trying to decide
whether the bullet wound in his head was self-inflicted
or whether he was a victim of violence.

Bascombe told reporters he was returning from getting a glass of beer on M Street. He had crossed the
bridge and was going down to board his oyster boat
when he heard someone running. He went up in time to
see a man run up the steps of the canal bridge. The man
wore a gray overcoat and no hat. It is assumed that this

is the man whose hat the police were hunting for until a late hour yesterday. A hat found at the scene (see picture of dog, page ten) was tentatively identified at the time by Miss Diane Hilyard, daughter of the dead dollar-a-year man, but turned out not to be Lawrason Hilyard's.

Bascombe stated that he identified the hatless man in the gray overcoat in the police line-up. Reporters were unable to learn his name. It is believed, however, that he was known to the dead metal king. Reporters questioning Bascombe were told that no one else was on the towing path at the assumed time of Mr. Hilyard's death. Bascombe heard a car start, but made no effort to investigate. He went directly to the police when he learned that a body had been found. He had not seen the early papers, having slept until noon on his boat on the river.

I sat there, my coffee untouched, getting stone-cold, staring stupidly down at the blurred type. My eyes focused again gradually and I looked at the picture under the article. It was gaily headed, NEED A HAT? and it showed a grinning policeman standing beside an enormous pile of male headgear of every possible description. There must have been nearly a hundred of them. WHAT WASHINGTON DOES WITH ITS CAST-OFF LIDS, it said underneath.

Police combing the canal and its environs found all these. It's an ill wind, as the old saying goes. They're going to be cleaned, blocked and sold for the benefit of Bundles for Bluejackets. A well-known local cleaner and dyer offered his services free as his contribution. First they'll be shown to Miss Diane Hilyard to see if she can identify the one she tossed out of her car window at the foot of Foxhall Road.

I turned the pages, glancing mechanically at the items I always read. At one of the gossip columns I stopped and looked again. It asked:

What's happened to Stanley Woland, who gave up his title and changed his name to become a democratic American? Rumors connecting him with a lovely heiress fell flat yesterday, and other rumors cropped up all over the place. An early phone call revealed he'd left town for an extended sojourn. Later inquirers were told he hadn't left town. Truth? Stanley has the mumps. Fate seems to be dogging the ex-glamour boy. It's particularly unkind just now when Stanley's well-known sympathetic manner might well have turned the trick.

I put the paper down. That column seemed so unnecessarily cruel that it was almost indecent. I felt beastly sorry for Stanley. I didn't want to see him marry Diane, but I didn't want him ruined either. And of course he simply had to stay in.

However, I thought, if he was on a spot, it was a lot better than the spot Bowen Digges was on.

13

I WAS GOING OVER ALL THAT IN MY
mind when the telephone rang. For a moment I didn't
get the name of the man who was speaking. Then I
understood it.

"Oh, good morning, Mr. Folger," I said.

"Will you lunch with me, Mrs. Latham?" he asked.
"On the Samarkand? It's my last party—I'm turning
her over to the Navy next week."

I hesitated. I could have told him I had a luncheon engagement, which was true, though I could beg
off. I was awfully curious about various things, but
still——

"My sister and the Eatons are going to be here,"
he went on. "My niece, Joan Eaton, thinks you've got
a pretty one-sided picture of the family from that little
wildcat of ours. It's all very quiet, of course, but it
would be a great pleasure——"

"Thank you," I said. "I'd like to. What time?"

"Could you make it about a quarter to one, or is
that too early?"

I put down the phone. I suppose I did have a one-

sided picture of the family, but I'd certainly got it
pretty directly from themselves, not Diane alone. It
would be interesting to see them when they weren't in
the same cage with their little wildcat. Maybe they
were very nice people. Still, it was odd, it seemed to me,
that they should have cared one way or the other about
what kind of a picture of them I'd got. It wasn't as
if they were staying in town and would have to go
on coping with me.

And it meant, of course, I was reflecting, that Mrs.
Hilyard had got safely back from her two-o'clock pilgrimage.

I was just wondering what I was going to say to
Colonel Primrose about the night before when Lilac
came up.

"The colonel he's downstairs," she announced. She
always does it, when there's trouble around, as if he'd
come in with the noose in his hand and was at that
moment engaged in erecting a gibbet in the front hall.

"Tell him I'll be down immediately," I said.

It was probably the hat, I thought. But it wasn't
the hat that I was worrying about just then. I had a
very real and intricate problem. I didn't care about
Mrs. Hilyard, but I did care about Diane and, in a
way, about the so-called beggar. I could still see his
face raised to the window, last Monday, when Mrs.
Hilyard peremptorily motioned her husband to go on.
The man might be cracked, I thought, but if more
people's religion gave them as sweet and other-worldly

a light in their eyes as his gave him, maybe more people would be handling out tracts and fewer ordnance supplies.

Colonel Primrose was standing in front of the fire reading the paper. He plainly hadn't had much sleep, and he also looked as if he wasn't in a mood to put up with anybody's being an obstructionist at that moment. He folded the paper and handed it to me.

"Have you seen this?"

It was the picture of all the hats. As I nodded I thought, *It's coming now.*

"If that hat turns up," he said, sitting down, "Mr. Bowen Digges' goose is very browned."

I didn't say anything. Neither did he for a moment.

"If I knew where it was, I'd have to turn it over to Lamb," he went on equably. "Fortunately, I don't."

I didn't look at him. "Would you suppose it might have been destroyed?"

"I hope not," he answered. "That would be damnably unfortunate. I expect that hat to be used in evidence, against Digges if he did murder Hilyard, or against whoever did do it."

"You're sure he was murdered?"

"I've never for an instant doubted it, my dear. There was no known reason for suicide. He had a mild peptic ulcer, but they tell me everybody in the Department of the Interior has that. They just attribute it to Mr. Ickes and go on a diet. Hilyard's letter of resignation, written after he got home from OPM, made an appointment for a board meeting tomorrow morning. Furthermore, he was in a rage when he left the house to take his dog out. A man doesn't start a suicidal depression that way."

"Do you know what he was in a rage about?" I asked.

He nodded. "I think so. It was partly one Mr. Ira Colton accusing him of holding out on promethium and ruining him, which is firmly and erroneously fixed in Mr. Ira Colton's mind. It was also partly his daughter Diane. According to Duncan Scott, the lawyer who was going to fix things for him, Colton lost his temper and told Hilyard a lot of things, including an item of gossip he'd picked up at a party."

"Was it about Stanley?" I asked quickly.

"About the five thousand dollars Stanley borrowed. And Stanley and Diane walked in nearly five minutes later."

"Oh, gosh," I said. "I suppose that was the door that hit Stanley, after all. Could he have done it?"

Colonel Primrose nodded calmly. "Stanley's life hasn't been designed to keep him particularly fit."

"So he was fibbing when he said Mr. Hilyard was pleased about having him for a son-in-law."

He looked at me with mild surprise. "Of course, Mrs. Latham. The law doesn't make a man give incriminating evidence against himself."

"Look," I said. "Is Bowen Digges really in such a mess?"

"I can think of one way it could be worse," he said soberly. "He could have been seen, by a reliable witness, with a gun in his hand, just before and immediately after it was fired at Hilyard's head."

"That was he in the police line-up, then?"

He nodded. "He says he doesn't remember running, but he was in a hurry and maybe he was. He won't say where he was running to, or why he was in a hurry."

He made a little gesture of impatience, as if Bowen Digges might have helped out with at least one explanation.

"And that's not all. He had appointments all day Tuesday. People sat around ten deep. And he never showed up. Lamb sent a man to OPM to pick up the washroom gossip. It seems he wasn't there, for one reason, because he'd gone somewhere the night before and got boiled to the eyebrows. Absolutely stinko."

"After he ran into Diane!" I said.

He nodded.

"Then he's still in love with her."

He drew a long breath. "I . . . should have thought you'd realized that," he said reproachfully. "Otherwise the fool would see the spot he's on. Well, Hilyard called him up when he didn't meet Duncan Scott and Colton for lunch and asked him to come to dinner before they came that night. He was all right by that time and said no, thanks, he'd be there at nine-twenty. He hung up the phone and said he might have to work with the hard-named old so-and-so, but he didn't have to eat with him. That was told around OPM before they'd heard about Hilyard."

"That was just dandy, wasn't it?" I said.

"It was mortar for the bricks, certainly." He got up and paced back and forth in front of the fire. "There are a lot of things I don't understand about this. Either it's the strangest series of coincidences or the young fellow is guilty. Lamb may be right, of course. He says I expect a person who's murdered somebody to cover up, and he points out that Digges did cover up. He made it look like suicide, and, as a matter of fact, that would have held if I hadn't happened to be interested in Hilyard before it happened."

He came back and sat down again.

"Lamb thinks he may still get away with it, if Mrs. Hilyard and the family stick to their story of suicide. But will they stick? They don't like Digges. If they realize the case against him, they may just quietly sign off and let him take it right on the chin."

"Oh, no!" I protested. "They couldn't do that."

He shrugged. "It's been done, Mrs. Latham. I don't mean they'd perjure themselves." He got up. "Digges' thumbprint is on the metal foil of that twisted cigarette pack, incidentally. There's a lot of circumstantial evidence about." He started to the door, stopped and came back. "Does anybody know where that hat is?" he asked gravely.

"Only the person who hid it, I suppose," I said. "Why?"

"Because I'd rather have Digges hanged, even if he's as innocent as an angel, than have anybody I care about pretty deeply get hurt because she's a quixotic, if very lovely, fool."

"I haven't the faintest idea what you're talking about, Colonel Primrose," I said.

He smiled. "Don't forget. I don't want anything to happen to it . . . or to you. Especially it."

I followed him out into the hall.

"What about the beggar?" I asked. I felt I was being awfully casual about it.

He looked at me.

"The mystery man, as the papers call him."

"What about him, my dear?" he asked placidly.

"I mean, has he been found yet?"

He shook his head. "We haven't got hold of him. I'll tell you about him later on."

He opened the door. Behind us the great granite form of Sgt. Phineas T. Buck was coming up out of the kitchen. He avoided looking at either of us, but at least he didn't spit.

I went back, got my coat and put on my galoshes to take Sheila for a walk to the market.

Lilac came heavily up the kitchen stairs. "The sergeant say the colonel ain' never goin' to solve no murders, nor nothin', if he keep on wastin' his time comin' over here irregardless."

I laughed. "You just tell the sergeant to mind his own business," I said.

" 'Deed Ah did. Ah tol' him we wouldn' give him or the colonel house room if you hadn' gone crazy as a June bug."

She normally used the more classical entomological phrase. I let it go at that and whistled for Sheila.

"When you goin' to remember to see 'bout my chair?" Lilac demanded darkly.

All my property is hers by definition. The chair was one I'd taken to the cabinetmaker's to be reglued a month before and forgotten all about.

"I'll do it now, Lilac," I said. I attached Sheila's leash, never dreaming that Lilac was the ebony fleshpot in which Fate had chosen to reside that morning.

14

MR. KALBFUS' SHOP IS IN AN OLD
shed and loft that was once the stable of one of those
red eighteenth-century Christmas-card houses that still
line Wisconsin Avenue. You get to it through a narrow
bricked passage, stumbling over garbage cans and
startled cats and uncollected milk bottles. The smell of
boiling fish glue and varnish remover is the only sign,
since LET KALBFUS FIX IT appeared last fall over the
game-room mantel of a well-known defense-contracts
lobbyist in Rock Creek Park.

I imagine there was an ostrich in Mr. Kalbfus' family tree. There's no other way to account for his extraordinary head, or for his disregard of the broken tables,
chairs and chests that sit around for months before he
gets to them. The head, looking like some very old,
long-buried egg, was bent over the gluepot when Sheila
and I came in.

"Lilac wants our chair, Mr. Kalbfus," I said. I could
see it under a great pile of other broken bits in the
corner against the rickety wall.

"Sit down, sit down," Mr. Kalbfus said. "You never

come to see me any more. That's why I keep your chair so long."

He pushed his big steel spectacles up on his bald old dome, wiped his hands on his leather apron, brushed the sawdust off his bench, reached for his blackened stump of a clay pipe and sat down. My chief reason for staying away, of course, was that nobody's work would ever get done if many people came in. I knew, however, that Mr. Kalbfus was not only by way of being a sage but was also a first-class cabinetmaker, whose family had been cabinetmakers before they came from Germany in 1848.

Then I noticed what he was working on. "Mr. Kalbfus!" I said. "Aren't you ashamed!"

I pointed to the armchair stuck rigidly in the vise at the other end of his bench. It was Mrs. Hilyard's.

"My chair's been here months!"

As a matter of fact, I was startled to see it. I was also very curious to know how she'd found Mr. Kalbfus in the first place. His old customers try to keep him for themselves.

"The lady had to have it right away," Mr. Kalbfus said, a little abashed. "She brought it in yesterday. She's leaving town right away. Right away. Someday, maybe, somebody's coming in and say, 'Mr. Kalbfus, I don't need this right away; I don't need it for three years.'" He wagged his head and chuckled. "Maybe. Maybe that's the end of the world I've been hearing about."

He pulled out a drawer full of big brass-headed up-holsterer's tacks and fished around in the back. I gave a very definite start this time. What he brought out was a little sheaf of the leaflets like the one Mrs. Hilyard had dropped the night before. I looked at the chair again, wondering.

Mr. Kalbfus put his spectacles back on and puffed at his pipe, sorting through them.

"Here's the one," he said. "The lion and the lamb will lie down together."

"Where did you get these, Mr. Kalbfus?" I asked.

"An old fellow wandered in here one morning, two, three weeks ago. He gave me one of these. We got to talking. He was all covered with snow, and he looked dead beat. I was trying to fix a brass lock on that tilt top over there. He knew all about it. Took off his coat and helped around all day. A first-class mechanic. About five he said he had to go. I said, 'Where are you stay-ing?' He said he had no place, so I said he could come back and stay here. I fixed him a mattress up in the loft. He's been here ever since."

"Oh," I said. "What's he like?"

Mr. Kalbfus tapped his forehead. "But the nicest old fellow you ever saw. He cleaned up, up there, and helped around. No trouble to anybody. I bring him over some coffee and bread in the morning. He goes out and peddles his little sermons and comes back and helps. Don't say much except when he gets on religion."

"Where is he from?" I asked.

"Never said, and I never asked." Mr. Kalbfus gently tapped the ashes out of his pipe. "Seems like he was wicked once. He did some fellow dirt, or some fellow did him dirt—I never made out. He's always talking in parables, like. Seems he's got to atone for whatever it was before Judgment Day. And that's just around the corner, like Prosperity. Well, everybody's got some kind of a knot in them, just like wood. Judgment Day's his, I reckon."

"Is he still here?"

"He hasn't come back, so far. Said, when he left, his work was almost finished. He only had a couple of things left to do."

I had a sinking feeling in the pit of my stomach.

"He was about out of pamphlets," Mr. Kalbfus said. "The only money he'd take from me was a dollar to get another batch. He wouldn't take any pay. The lady that brought that chair saw the ones I had, and she left him an envelope with a dollar in it yesterday evening. I thought it was right nice of her. I expect that's why I'm doing her chair so quick."

"Did he go out much at night?"

Mr. Kalbfus shook his head. "I don't know. I let him make a key the second day he was around. He was real handy like that. He just came and went. Such a nice old fellow, I liked having him around."

I hesitated a minute. Then I said, "The police have been hunting for him for a couple of days. Don't you read the papers?"

He shook his head again. "No, I don't read the papers. All that's in them is war, war, trouble, trouble, hurry, rush, right away, right away. There's too many newspapers and too many radios. I don't pay any attention to either one. My customers tell me all I need to hear."

He reached for a knife and started digging around the bowl of his pipe.

"So the police are after him. They're always after somebody that's not doing anybody any harm. When somebody stole my sign, they didn't do anything at all. One of my customers saw it and told me about it. I told the police. One of them brought me around ten dollars and said the party that had it wanted to keep it, and he was a big shot, so he was paying me instead. I gave it to the first poor old nigger woman that came along. But they're hot after an old lunatic that don't do any harm except pestering people about the hereafter, because nobody wants to think about that these days."

I didn't see any point in telling him why they wanted his lodger, or, what he also apparently didn't know, that the woman who wanted her chair right away was in the newspapers too. I picked up Sheila's leash. He came to the door with us.

"I'll get your chair right away," he said.

"Any time will do."

I decided, on my way home, to tell Colonel Primrose, but not the police. Mr. Kalbfus wouldn't tell them, I was sure of that. Colonel Primrose was different. He understood odd and simple people, and he had a genuine respect for the rights of man that a uniform seems to dull in some people. I called him up as soon as I got in the house, but he was out. I called again twice before I went down to the Samarkand to lunch with Bartlett Folger and the Hilyards.

I did leave a message with Lilac to tell him I had some news, if he called; but I should have stopped by his house and left a note. It didn't seem that important or that immediate just then. I've tried to tell myself it was Fate, just as it was Fate that took me into Mr. Kalbfus' shop that morning. But mostly I try not to think of it at all, especially when I wake up in the middle of the night and can't go back to sleep.

I nosed my car into the iron fence in the parking space at the end of the fish market on Twelfth and Maine Avenue. Ahead of me to the left, a couple of blocks back across a narrow ribbon of water, I could see the columns and low flat rotunda of the new Jefferson Memorial. On the right, above the long roof of the market warehouse, the Washington Monument gleamed stark and foreshortened in the winter sunlight. The clock on the octagonal brick tower said twenty minutes to one as I got out and made my way across the wharf.

A few hardy people were eating lunch outside on the narrow balcony of a sea-food restaurant upstairs in the market, and a bug-eye, painted blue and pink, was lying in the slip. Beyond it and the oystermen and the colored boys shucking oysters, at a farther dock out in another world where no fish smelled, lay the yacht Samarkand,

trim and white and lovely against the silver stretch of
the Potomac and the flat snow-covered expanse of Hains
Point, its graceful willows etched sharply against the
winter sky. I went on board. A servant took my coat,
said, "Just here, madam," and led me to a mahogany
door at the end of a narrow corridor. I went into a
charming paneled room with a wood fire burning on
the hearth, and gay with flowers and chintz.

The abrupt silence that met me was certainly neither
charming nor gay. It was as cold as the piles of rock
salt and chipped ice that I'd passed behind the market
stalls. What I'd innocently run in on had not been just
friendly chitchat. I found myself facing the exceed-
ingly solid back of a tall young man in a tweed coat and
gray flannel trousers, who'd evidently been doing the
listening, with my host, Bartlett Folger, facing him,
doing the talking. It was a kind of instantaneous still-
ness that lasted only that long before it broke and the
young man wheeled around. It was Bowen Digges.

Mr. Folger recovered himself sharply and came forward, smiling, his hand open.

"This is splendid," he said. "How do you do, Mrs.
Latham? This is Mr. Digges."

Bowen Digges hadn't quite the social presence of my
host. It took him definitely longer to say, "How do you
do?" which he did eventually with a kind of guarded
ease that was non-committal in the extreme. I saw he
was wondering what I was doing there. I suppose it was
fair enough, as I was doing the same about him.

Bartlett Folger turned back to him. "We'll finish

this another time, Bowen. My guests are due just now."

Mr. Bowen Digges didn't move except to take out a cigarette and light it. There was an electric crackle in the air.

"I . . . think not," he said coolly. "Your other guests can wait a minute, Mr. Folger. I'd like you to go on. It so happens that Mrs. Latham is one of the people who heard about it. She might be as interested as I am."

He turned politely to me.

"You see, I've now been told three times (a) that Mr. Hilyard offered me twenty-five hundred dollars to get out of town because he didn't want his daughter to marry me, and (b) that I accepted with thanks. As neither one happens to be so, I've decided I'd like to get things straight." He turned back to Bartlett Folger. "From the horse's mouth, so to speak."

I thought Mr. Folger looked a little irritated in spite of his great self-possession.

"All right," he said. "I don't think Mrs. Latham can be very much interested in your problems, frankly ——"

"This is your problem, Mr. Folger," Bowen said.

I resisted the temptation to say that I was interested, very much indeed.

Bartlett Folger went on, choosing his words carefully. "I admit it's unfortunate it happened. At the time none of us had any idea you had the stuff in you to do the job you've done. What you've——"

"We can skip that," Bowen said. "You have guests coming."

Mr. Folger nodded. "My sister and brother-in-law thought Diane was too young to marry."

"We weren't planning to get married for some years," Bowen said. "But go on."

Bartlett Folger glanced at him, his face flushing a little. "You ought to understand," he said coolly, "that they thought you were a smart-aleck young pup trying to marry a rich girl. And Diane's as headstrong and stubborn as a——"

"What's that about me?"

I hadn't heard the door open. Diane Hilyard was standing there with her back to it, her hand still on the knob. She had on a tweed coat and a tan sweater and plaid skirt, with tan socks and brown-and-white saddle shoes, and she was hatless, as usual, and infinitely at ease.

She didn't look at either Bowen Digges or me.

"Go on, Uncle Bart," she said calmly.

"I forgot to tell you, Mr. Folger," Bowen said, "that I asked Diane to come around. I wanted her to get this straight too."

He said it easily, but not so easily as he'd spoken before. She did something to him that tightened his face and made his voice almost harsh.

It was a lovely yacht we were on, I thought, but at that moment I didn't envy Mr. Bartlett Folger in the least. Personally, I would just as soon have had a tank brigade facing me as those two perfectly composed and level-eyed youngsters standing there waiting for him to go on.

I thought Mr. Folger was thinking something of the sort too.

"This is ... pretty tough on me," he said sardonically. "I didn't have anything to do with it, except to soften the blow as much as I could. I thought the thing would die a natural death. The family were for kicking you out. We decided to put it on a different basis. You'd been puttering around the laboratory and you'd rigged up a filter that was better than the one we had. I suggested to my brother-in-law that while we weren't under any obligation to pay you for it, since it was done on our time, he could make it the excuse to pay you and let you out without too much of an injustice. It was worth about two hundred dollars, as you probably know now."

Bowen Digges was staring at him very steadily. He hadn't even looked at Diane.

"It would have been worth more if I'd patented it," he said coolly.

"It wasn't yours to patent."

Bowen nodded. "I guess you're right. I probably owe you a lot more than twenty-five hundred for letting me have the run of the lab. I couldn't have got in Tech if I hadn't had that behind me."

He stood there silently for a moment. I looked at Diane Hilyard. She was still there by the door. The corners of her red mouth were drawn down and her eyes were fastened on the floor, two dull spots burning in her cheeks under the long sweep of her eyelashes.

"And so the truth is," Bowen Digges said quietly, "that I really was paid twenty-five hundred dollars, not for my filter, but to get out of town."

"If you want to put it that way."

"Is there any other way to put it?"

"Then that's it," Bartlett Folger said coolly. "I'm sorry if it——"

"Oh, on the contrary," Bowen said. There was a kind of grim cheerfulness in his voice. "It's my own fault. I should have known the Promethium Corporation wasn't handing over twenty-five hundred dollars for something they could have for nothing. I'm just a—a little surprised that I wasn't bright enough to see it without having to be hit over the head. I must have given you all a good belly laugh. All the time I was swallowing the home-town-boy-makes-good stuff. Glad he can enlarge his opportunities in a broader field. Well, it certainly had me buffaloed."

His laugh had some genuine amusement in it. I looked at Diane again. The spots in her cheeks were hotter and brighter. Her eyes were smoldering, ready to burst into blue flame.

"And just to show you I don't mind," he went on, "I'll tell you I had it all figured out that my filter must be damned good, worth at least twenty-five thousand, for you to loosen up on twenty-five hundred. I did you an injustice, and I apologize."

"You don't have to say 'you,'" Folger said, with some irritation. "I didn't have anything to do with it, except . . . try to make it easier. I'm glad it helped you to go on and make something of yourself."

"Thanks a lot," Bowen said.

"There's no use of your getting sore about it."

"Oh, I'm not sore at you." He couldn't have been calmer. "I'm sore at myself, for being such a bloody fool. After Diane let me down, it came as a sop to the ego. I wasn't good enough for her or the family. Carey Eaton was, but not me. Nevertheless, something I'd worked out was good enough to be used in the factory, and good enough to make you disgorge twenty-five hundred bucks. Carey couldn't do that. So it's a little tough to find it was—let's say charity, or hush money. On the whole, I'd rather have had a plain kick in the pants. I don't like fancy ones."

He hadn't looked at Diane since she'd come in, and he didn't look at her now.

"So go ahead, all of you. Tell everybody you paid me to get out and I was glad to settle. I'd rather people would think I'm a louse instead of a cockeyed fool." He took a couple of steps toward the door. "I trust you still think in terms of six per cent," he said coolly. "I'll get a check to you, for Mr. Hilyard's estate, this afternoon. If I have to beg, borrow or steal it."

Diane Hilyard moved aside from the door.

"So I will run along," Bowen said. He closed the door behind him.

Diane looked up at her uncle. I've never seen such burning scorn in anybody's face.

"Just a minute, Diane," he said. "You don't understand. Your father and mother——"

"I understand all I need to," she said. The contempt in her voice was like a thin rawhide lash drawn across his face. "You lied to him, and you've lied to me for years—you and my father and my mother, and Joan and Carey. They knew, too, didn't they? Every one of you." The whole room seemed to vibrate with her low, passionate accusal. "What else did you tell him? He said, when I 'let him down.' That's something else you've done. No wonder my father wouldn't let me know he was here. And all the rest of you. I don't believe now you didn't know. I won't believe anything any one of you ever tells me, ever again. No wonder my father wanted to resign and go back home. He was the only one of you with decency enough to be ashamed of himself. I don't wonder you didn't want me here to lunch. I don't see how any one of you can bear to have me around at all!"

She put her hand on the doorknob. Her uncle took a step forward.

"Oh, I'm not going to run after him and ask him what it was you told him!" she said hotly. "I'm too ashamed of the Hilyards ever to ask him to speak to one of them again! He can go on thinking I'm as contemptible as the rest of you! It's what I deserve for being one of you!"

She went quickly to the window. I looked out. Bowen Digges was striding across the concrete pavement on the wharf, toward his car. I could see Diane's face crumple a little as she turned her head quickly to hide it from her uncle. She looked out again. Suddenly her hand tightened on the low back of the easy chair at her side and her body went taut.

A man had come out from behind the small white brick outbuilding there and was coming slowly toward Bowen. It was Mrs. Hilyard's beggar, Mr. Kalbfus' solitary lodger. Bowen Digges glanced at him and strode on. The man raised his hand to stop him, and followed slowly along. As Bowen reached his car and opened the door, he glanced back. The man was walking toward him more quickly.

Bartlett Folger had come to the window. "Isn't that the fellow the police are hunting for?" he asked. "The one that's been hanging around Prospect Street?"

Neither Diane nor I said anything. He went quickly around the table and reached for the telephone. "What's the police number, Mrs. Latham?"

"You dial the operator and say, 'I want a policeman,'" Diane said coolly.

I saw her reach her foot out, press the toe of her shoe on the cord under the table, and jerk the plug sharply out of the socket onto the rug.

"This damned phone's dead!" Bartlett Folger exclaimed. He jiggled the bar rapidly for a moment, slammed the receiver down and started for the door.

"It's too late," Diane said. "He's gone. Bowen's gone too. And I'm going. Good-by." She closed the door behind her.

Mr. Folger stood silently at the corner of the yellow marble hearth for a moment. Then he looked at me.

"I'm sorry you were let in on this, Mrs. Latham."

I couldn't think of a thing to say. In a sense, I was sorry too.

"Well, it's all come home to roost," he continued. "There was no use lying to her in the beginning. And there's no use now."

I didn't understand him for a moment. "You mean you are still doing it?" I asked then.

"I've been opposed to it from the beginning," he said slowly. "There's never any use trying to save people anything. Let them take it and put up with it. It's better in the long run."

"What do you mean?" I asked. "Are you saving somebody something?"

As it appeared to me, the only need of saving—or face-saving—was for themselves and their own treachery to Diane and Bowen Digges.

"Diane," he said. "We've been trying to save her another shock."

"I don't understand you, Mr. Folger," I said.

He looked at me for an instant. "If the police don't find that Lawrason shot himself," he said deliberately, "they'll find it was Bowen Digges that did. That's what we've been trying to save Diane . . . to try to make up for all the rest of it. Lawrason is dead. Nothing can bring him back again."

I was staring at him with a sick kind of unbelief.

"What do you mean?" I asked. "That's a terrible thing to say, unless you know."

"He was on the towing path with him Tuesday night."

"That doesn't mean he shot him!" I said sharply.

"Bowen Digges was standing by my brother-in-law earlier that night," he said coolly, "watching him sign a release he'd brought. The desk drawer was open. The gun Lawrason was shot with was lying in it. Digges picked it up and said, 'This is a neat little job, Mr. Hilyard. There are some people I'd just as soon use it on, myself.' There were three people in the room then. None of them saw him put it back. One of them saw him slip it into his pocket."

"Who . . . was that?" I managed to ask.

"My niece's husband, Carey Eaton," he said.

15

"You're all willing to perjure yourselves, then, just to keep Diane from knowing?" I asked. Somehow, I couldn't see Carey Eaton, at least, in such a role to save anybody, least of all Diane Hilyard.

Bartlett Folger moved abruptly, as if he wanted to get physically away from that implication. He reached for a cigarette off the coffee table in front of us.

"It sounds unpleasant, put that way. In fact, it's not pleasant any way you put it. I suppose the least unpleasant way is to say that it's an atonement." He stopped and looked at me in surprise. "What's the matter? Isn't that a good word?"

"It's a very good word," I said. "I was just startled at hearing you use it."

I looked out of the cabin window. A policeman was standing by the passage through the lower story of the market, talking to a uniformed marine on duty.

The composite picture of Mr. Kalbfus' lodger couldn't be out yet, I thought.

"If I talk about atonement, Mrs. Latham, I suppose

I ought to say we all sinned in this. My sister was ambitious, so was Joan. The idea of Diane marrying Bowen was a jolt to everybody. You can't see that now, after what he's become, but he was pretty callow then. I imagine you know about his family."

I nodded.

"And Carey was going in the plant. He's all right now, but he was a snob then if I ever saw one. You wouldn't recognize him as the same person."

"I'm not sure," I said. "But do go on."

He hesitated an instant. "I might as well tell you about it, since you've stumbled in on it. Everybody was upset. Joan wouldn't marry Carey if Diane was going to disgrace everybody, and so on. And Diane was only seventeen. Nobody thought she really loved the boy. Lawrason thought of her as a baby, still, and so did I. I didn't want him kicked out, because he was a good man. And I still don't know whether Joan and Carey did it as a joke or from malice."

He got up and looked out of the window.

"They ought to be here any minute. . . . Well, Diane had a typewriter. She'd saved the money out of her allowance to get it. She was teaching herself to type. The idea was to get a job and help Bowen go to college. She had it hidden under her bed. Joan found it, and she and Carey wrote a letter on it." Mr. Folger shook his head. "With all the stumbling mistakes, and so on. It was pretty cruel."

"I can imagine so," I said.

"It was something to the effect that she'd decided it was too hard work learning to type, and that washing dishes and learning how to run a gas pump would be harder. Well, it was . . . pretty bad. They didn't mean Bowen to see it, I'm sure of that. I suppose they thought it would open Diane's eyes. Anyway, a maid found it and gave it to my sister. She thought Diane had written it, and Lawrason called Bowen in and gave it to him."

"How horrible!" I said.

He nodded coolly. "I know. Well, that was where I came in. Bowen was still coming to work. He was puttering around with some experiment. That didn't work out either, and that was almost as hard on him. What with one and the other, he was going around half stunned. That was when I persuaded Hilyard to call him in and give him enough to get him away. We knew he wouldn't take it as a gift or a loan, which is where the idea of paying for the filter came in."

I must have just sat there staring at him, I suppose.

"And do you mean that the Eatons didn't ever do anything about the letter?"

"You've never seen Diane when she's angry, Mrs. Latham. Or Digges. Or Lawrason Hilyard, for that matter."

"Did they tell you about it?"

He shook his head. "When Joan had her baby, they didn't think she'd pull through. She told her mother about it then, and her mother told me. They thought

Diane would get over it, and someday they could tell her for their own piece of mind."

"And that's just dandy," I said. "But it doesn't help any, does it?"

"No. And you see why they—and all of us—are willing to perjure ourselves, as you call it."

"To save Carey and Joan Eaton," I said. "After all, if Bowen knew this, or Diane——"

"God help us," Bartlett Folger said soberly.

"Did Mr. Hilyard know?"

He shook his head again. "He was a ruthless fellow, but he was scrupulously honorable in his personal relations. He was really fond of Diane—she was the only thing he did love. He hated dogs, for instance, but he'd take that little beast of hers out. And you can see what a mixup it was. He thought she'd written the letter. Digges pulled out without a word, of course. Diane went around to his mother before she finally picked up and moved the rest of the family. I don't know what Bowen had told her, but Diane changed completely. She just closed up a large part of herself. Lawrason thought she was being difficult. He didn't want to tell her, naturally, that they'd read a letter she'd written. One day he got angry with her and pulled out the cancelled check. She just looked at it for a minute and walked out. She was so matter-of-fact about it that he didn't realize for a long time what it had done to her. Then it was too late."

"A Hilyard never retracts," I said.

"A Hilyard, or a Folger, or an Eaton," he said coolly. "Especially if it's going to mean discomfort to themselves."

"So that——"

"Here they come," he said. "You know, I wanted to tell you this; that's why I asked you to come early. I wanted you to know something about Diane and her family. You can see why she's never to know any of this."

"Yes, I think I can," I replied. "From her point of view, as well as the rest of the Hilyards and the Folgers and the Eatons." I didn't add "the Diggeses."

"You can also see what I mean by 'atonement,' as opposed to the word you used. 'Perjury,' wasn't it?"

I suppose I was looking at Mrs. Hilyard and the Eatons with a new set of eyes that afternoon. I was even prepared to have a kind of dubious sympathy for Carey and Joan. Bartlett Folger's story being true— and I hadn't any reason to think it wasn't—they had played a filthy and unpardonable trick on Diane. But from what I'd seen and heard, I couldn't imagine they'd put much in the letter that they hadn't said to her face, one time or another. Moreover, I could believe it was true they hadn't intended Bowen Digges ever to see it, just because I doubted if either of them would care to run the risk. The thing had backfired, with consequences that neither of them had the courage or the decency to face, and that wasn't too hard to understand.

Furthermore, it might even be true that they really

were trying to atone for it, as Bartlett Folger said, by shielding Bowen Digges. Or thinking they were shielding him, I added to myself. However, I always suspect the shining White Knight rising like a phoenix from the ashes, and, as far as I could see, a new nobility of soul hadn't improved Mr. Carey Eaton much.

It was easy to see how he had impressed both his wife and her mother, then and now.

He· was very good-looking indeed, with black hair and black eyes; broad-shouldered, perfectly groomed, beautifully tailored, and well aware of all of it. I'd seldom seen such a spoiled young man. But of course that might be the fault of circumstances. His wife and mother-in-law certainly contributed their share.

He took the cocktail a servant held out to him and sniffed at it.

"You ought to teach that man of yours to make a decent Martini, Uncle Bart," he said.

Joan Eaton smiled at him. "We only know two houses in Washington where Carey will touch the Martinis," she said. "It's frightfully embarrassing."

Her expression seemed, to me, to show pride in his connoisseurship rather than anything else. I looked at her curiously. It was hard to believe she was really Diane's sister. Her eyes and hair were dark brown and her figure stocky compared to Diane's, and she was carefully and smartly dressed, in one of those little black numbers that cost a lot of money.

Bartlett Folger smiled. "What about you, Mrs. Latham?"

"It tastes fine to me," I replied. "But of course my standards are Washingtonian and pretty low."

Carey Eaton raised his glass and got the Martini down without visible gagging.

"Who is this Colonel Primrose that's about?" he asked.

Both the question and the manner in which it was asked stopped me for an instant.

"Where'd he get the 'colonel'?" he went on. "South'n governor's staff?"

I shook my head. "Regular Army. Last war. He was raised on active duty, and kept his rank."

He looked at me oddly for an instant. "That's . . . funny. I called up the War Department and they'd never heard of him."

"Oh, well," I said, "there are so many retired colonels around."

"I had to tell him that when authorized authorities wanted to know my timing and whereabouts Tuesday night, I'll be happy to tell them."

It was my turn to look at him oddly.

"I thought he was official," Bartlett Folger said. "When did you see him?"

"This noon."

We'd gone in to lunch.

"I did tell him, of course, that we all had dinner here with you, Uncle Bart, and took father home in time for a nine-o'clock appointment. I don't know what time the rest of you got home."

"I thought we told you," Mr. Folger said with a smile.

I was just getting the impression that it was going to be a dull luncheon, when two things happened.

Joan Eaton turned to me. "It was very strange, Mrs. Latham," she said. "It proves there's something. It wasn't a premonition exactly, but we were sitting in there. Mother felt sick, all of a sudden. I looked at the clock, and mentioned it was twenty-five minutes after eleven. I asked mother if she hadn't better lie down or should we go home. That was just about——"

"It was twenty-five minutes to twelve that it happened," Mrs. Hilyard said quietly.

"Well, that's just ten minutes' difference. I told Carey about it when he came in."

Mr. Folger was in the process of taking a stuffed squab from the silver platter held down to him. I saw his hands stay motionless for the barest instant.

"I . . . thought you were home, when I left you."

"I was," Carey Eaton said. "One of the men on Export Control called me up at eleven-thirty, furthermore, to check on a permit they wanted to issue right away."

In the hush that had fallen in the room for just an instant, Mr. Folger turned to his sister.

"By the way, Myrtle, that beggar was around here this morning. I called the——" He broke off abruptly. If a bomb had dropped into the center of the table, the effect on Mrs. Hilyard could hardly have been more terrible. Her fork slipped out of her hand and clattered across her plate onto the floor. She stared at her brother, her lips open, her face as white as the luncheon cloth. She was leaning back in her chair in almost abject shock and fear.

Joan got up quickly and went to her.

Mrs. Hilyard struggled to her feet.

"I—— Excuse me, please," she managed to say.

Carey Eaton helped her to the door, Joan following.

Mr. Folger and I looked at each other.

"Well," he said. "I'm sorry, Mrs. Latham."

He pushed back his chair and I got up quickly. I'd had plenty—of food and everything else. "I think I'd better go, Mr. Folger. I have an engagement at three, and it's——"

Carey had come back. "I've got to get to the office too," he said curtly. "Can I drop you anywhere, Mrs. Latham?"

"Thanks, I've got my car," I answered. I had the grim feeling that if Carey Eaton dropped me anywhere just then, it would be down a manhole when my back was turned.

16

THERE WAS A NOTE ON MY DESK WHEN
I got home. "The colonel was here an' lef' it," Lilac
said, pointing it out to me.

I opened it. It was hastily scribbled on a sheet of my
house paper.

Mrs. Latham: Will you see if you can get hold of
B. D. and ask him to come in for a drink this afternoon,
late, and keep him here under some pretext—if any is
needed—until I come? This is getting serious. I'm trying to avoid publicity as long as I can. His number is
Republic 7500.   J. P.

An added line at the bottom read:

I believe I was right about the family. The wind is
shifting.

I read it through again and dropped it into the fire.
The last line stood out clear and distinct on the blackened paper before the flames gulped it down. I stood

there wondering about it, unable to think of it except in terms of Carey Eaton. He was the one member of the family Colonel Primrose had seen that day, so far as I knew, since he'd talked to me. And all I could think about it was that he'd been very pointed about his alibi, at lunch, and that he was the one who'd seen Bowen Digges pick up the gun there in the Hilyard library Tuesday night.

I dialed Republic 7500. Bowen was pretty well protected at OPM. I had to give my name, tell why I wanted to speak to him, and a good deal more, before I could get hold of him.

When I did, and explained it again, he said, "I'd like to come, if I'm not in jail." Then he hesitated. "Wait a minute. Is anybody else going to be there?"

"Not unless you'd like me to ask her," I answered.

He made a sound that could have been mistaken for a laugh, but not very easily.

"No, I'm afraid I couldn't take it. Not just now."

It was quarter to six when he came. The evening papers were out, of course, and a kind of perspective had been re-established. Men dying in the Pacific were more important again than the man who'd died in the C. & O. Canal. Only one column on the front page was given to Lawrason Hilyard. POLICE REPORT PROGRESS, REFUSE DETAILS, it said. I looked through it hastily. The chief of the homicide squad, Captain Lamb, stated that several members of the family of the dollar-a-year OPM man had been recalled for questioning. Captain

Lamb had refused to comment on the rumor circulating at OPM that a member of the division of which Mr. Hilyard had been chief had been taken to headquarters and grilled for several hours. Lamb said everyone known to have had any association with the dead magnate would be questioned, but refused to name any individual or comment on names suggested by reporters. He admitted that no progress had been made in the police search for a man seen around the Prospect Street mansion.

It went on with a résumé of the case on an inside page. When I turned it I started violently. Bowen Digges' picture covered several columns above it. The implication didn't need to be stated.

LONG MENTIONED TO REPLACE DEAD OPM CHIEF, it said at the top. Under that I read in boldface type:

It was disclosed today that Bowen Digges, assistant chief of the Promethium Division of OPM, has taken charge until a successor can be appointed. It is also stated that Carey Eaton, the dead promethium magnate's son-in-law, may be called in to head the division. He has been connected with the Promethium Corporation for the last five years and is familiar with both defense needs and the available supply.

It also became known today that Digges, the acting head, was at one time employed in a minor position in the plant of the dead man whose position he now holds. An ill-fated romance, it is said, was responsible for his breaking his connection with the corporation several years ago. No confirmation of this could be secured. The dead division chief had two daughters. One is Mrs. Carey Eaton, whose husband may succeed her father. The other is Miss Diane Hilyard, whose name has been romantically connected, recently, with Stanley Woland, the former Count Stanislaus Wolanski.

I'd just finished reading it when Bowen came in.

"Hullo," he said. "Nice of you to ask me." He glanced at the paper lying on the sofa. "I'm beginning to think I ought to carry a little bell around. The leper's spots are beginning to show. Or am I mixed up?" He held his hands out to the fire. "If they don't put me in jail pretty soon, I'm going to have to buy another overcoat."

"If they wait, you'll die of pneumonia, and save the taxpayers' money."

"The Diggeses are tough," he said. "You'd be surprised." He looked at the paper again. "But not tough enough. I guess they couldn't keep it out any longer."

"I suppose not," I agreed.

He slumped down in the wing chair by the corner of the hearth and sat there silently. His face had sobered into hard clean lines. There wasn't a flaccid muscle or drooping line in it. It wasn't handsome, as Carey Eaton's was, but it was better. It had strength and character. It was the fundamental difference between them, just as it was between Diane and her sister Joan.

I mixed him a Scotch and soda and took it over to him.

"You didn't shoot Mr. Hilyard, did you, Mr. Digges?" I asked, going back and sitting down again.

He grinned irrepressibly then. "I'll shoot you if you call me Mr. Digges again, Mrs. Latham."

"All right," I said. "But you didn't, did you?"

He looked at me thoughtfully. "Shoot Hilyard?"

I nodded.

"No," he said. "I didn't. But if I'd known what Folger told me this noon, I certainly would have."

"I'd shut up about it, in that case."

"Why? If they're going to hang me anyway, I might as well get it off my chest while I'm still here. I don't expect to meet any of them on the other side. I may go to hell, but I won't be in the bottom pit."

"You're just going to sit around and let them hang you, I take it."

"Not on your life," he said evenly. "Not if I can help it, I'm not. But it's beginning to look as if there's not so much I can do about it."

"You can explain where you got all that blood on your clothes, for one thing," I said. "Have you got some quixotic idea of saving somebody, or something?"

"Just myself," he said calmly. "No, that's one satisfaction I won't give them."

There was a bitterness in his voice that surprised me.

"Give who?"

"The Hilyards."

He leaned forward, looking down into the fire.

"It's a funny thing," he said.

"What is?"

"Ever since I was a kid, the Hilyards have dominated my life, in one way or another. It's hard to explain if you've never lived in a one-family town. Everything was by the grace of the Hilyards—politics, jobs, everything. My father worked in the plant. He was killed there. I worked there; one of my brothers. My mother never wanted to stay, but she had to. Well, I never wanted to leave. And then, later, I never wanted to see or hear of one of them again." He picked up his glass and put it down again. "I was free of them for five years. Except for one. And that was the bitterest of the lot."

I hadn't realized how deep that wound had been, how sore and sensitive it still was. He'd covered up, the three times I'd seen them together. It wasn't covered up now.

"In a way, it was all right, I guess. I worked like the devil to try to forget it, and to—to show them. I took a lot of exams and got in Tech as a special student. My mother'd been a school-teacher, and the work in the plant laboratory helped a lot. I worked nights in a service station for six months. Then things picked up. I made it in two years, and the last three I've been teaching and working in metallurgy. If you work hard enough, and long enough hours, you can forget . . . almost anything." He gave me a kind of a grin. "How'd

I get on this subject? Anyway, when they asked me to come here in the minor metals, I went to a lot of pains to make sure none of the Hilyards were going to be around. Then in a couple of months I was transferred to promethium and Hilyard showed up as a dollar-a-year man."

He stopped a moment.

"It was a funny thing. I was going to resign and get out. Then I ran into him accidentally. We'd both changed. He was a pretty big frog, of course, but this pond's huge, and he was jittery. Well, I found I didn't care any more. The job was too big. We were doing two important sides of it. And we got along all right. It was absolutely impersonal; you'd never have known we'd ever met before."

I deliberately said, "Did you know when Diane came?"

"I heard him talk to her on the phone one day. She was waiting in her car to meet him one day when I came out. Well, it wasn't so easy after that. I realized it wasn't the family; it was just old . . . hurt. . . . I guess I'm being a bloody fool." He finished his drink. "Anyway, I've got to be going. I'm boring the socks off you."

I looked desperately at the clock. It was well after six, and no sign of Colonel Primrose.

"You haven't told me what you are going to do to keep from being hanged," I said.

I wanted very much to tell him about Diane and that letter, but I didn't dare.

"I didn't shoot Hilyard," he said. "He was alive when I left him. And he certainly didn't give me the impression he had any idea of killing himself. That's rot. Somebody did it—and I can think of a lot of people, and a lot of reasons. I've gone on saying I hated his guts—I said that to you—but, as a matter of fact, it wasn't true any longer. It was just force of habit." He shook his head. "I wish to God I knew who did it. It's got me wondering, sometimes, if I went crazy and did it myself."

There was a kind of pain in his voice that frightened me. Otherwise I don't think I'd have said what I did.

"What about that old man, Bowen?"

He looked up at me. "What old man?"

"The one the police are hunting for. He was hanging around Prospect Street. Mrs. Hilyard told me he's a beggar. But there's something queer about that. He's been living over at an antique-repair shop back off Wisconsin Avenue, Mrs. Kalbfus' place, and Mr. Kalbfus told me he won't even take money for the work he does. He distributes leaflets about the end of the world."

Bowen shook his head. "I read about him in the papers. I know the type, and I know the place, but I don't know him. He doesn't mean anything to me."

"I thought you recognized him today," I said.

He stared at me. "What do you mean?"

"Down on the wharf. When you left the boat. He came out——"

I didn't get any further. The slowly changing expression on his face stopped me. It shifted gradually, as he sat there staring at me, from surprise to incomprehension to a sudden understanding, and then to something else that I couldn't name. And then Mr. Bowen Digges leaped to his feet.

"Magnussen!" he shouted. "I thought I knew that fellow!"

He was across the room before I could catch my breath. At the door he whirled around. "Bless you, Mrs. Latham!"

I heard the front door slam.

17

I WAITED TWENTY-FIVE MINUTES from the time Bowen Digges hurtled out, slamming the door, till Colonel Primrose, in his usual quiet and deliberate way, sort of hurtled in, slamming the door. He clearly expected Bowen to be there.

"He did come, but he left," I explained calmly. "Mrs. Hilyard's beggar is named Magnussen, and Bowen knows him. I told him where he'd been staying. He dashed out before I could move, much less stop him."

He stood there staring at me. Then he took a deep, steadying breath. I think he would have been very glad to throttle me.

"Why didn't you tell me instead?"

"I tried to. You were out and I couldn't get hold of you."

"Where is he?"

"Magnussen? He's been staying with Mr. Kalbfus, where I take my furniture to be repaired. Do you want me to show you?" I was getting a little frightened.

"Quickly," he answered.

"It's quicker to walk," I said.

We set out. I guess I don't know him very well, because I'd never thought I'd have to lope, practically, to keep up with him.

"Now let's have it," he said.

The sidewalk was uneven and icy, and I stumbled along, trying to tell him, as briefly as I could, about going into Mr. Kalbfus' and seeing the chair and the leaflets. I told him about what Mr. Kalbfus had said, and about my seeing the old man at the wharf, and Bowen's not recognizing him until I mentioned him half an hour before.

"There's more of it; I'll tell you," I said. "It's just down there."

We were on the broader main drag of Georgetown, crossing over through the home-coming traffic behind a line of streetcars waiting at the switch. It seemed more congested than usual. And I felt Colonel Primrose's hand on my arm tighten sharply.

Ahead of us at the passage was a crowd of people, of all gradations between solid black and deathly white, and the deathliest white was my friend, Mr. Kalbfus, half standing and half supported by two outsize policemen.

I was shocked and frightened. "Oh, do something, quick!" I said. "That's Mr. Kalbfus; he's an angel!"

"I wish you'd thought of that sooner," he said. He hurried along.

Mr. Kalbfus gave me a sick, pleading look as we went by.

A policeman at the dark narrow tunnel between the houses pushed people away. "Get back there. Let the colonel in."

A garbage can had been knocked over in the passage. I followed Colonel Primrose through the mess, pushing the can out of the way and stumbling over the top, back into the open yard. The shed was lighted. The feeble yellow glow coming through the windows elongated the dark figures of men milling about in the littered garden.

A policeman came to meet us. "No place for a lady, sir," he said grimly.

The hysterical thought flashed into my head that Colonel Primrose was going to say, "That ain't no lady, and it ain't my wife."

Instead, he said, "Wait here," and went quickly to the door. The men inside moved away, and I saw him. I knew already, of course, so it shouldn't have been the awful shock it was. It must have just happened. His body was still lying, motionless and limp, across Mr. Kalbfus' workbench, the old rocking chair he'd been sitting in kicked over on its side. His spectacles were hanging on one ear, his Bible had fallen face down on the dirty floor, some of its thin leaves curled under. The whole back of his skull was a terrible crushed mass.

I saw Colonel Primrose looking down at the iron weight lying on the floor, stained dark and still moist. But that wasn't all I saw. Bowen was standing at the end of the table, his face drawn and greenish-gray. He was holding on to a chair. It struck me as horribly ironic in some way that it was my chair—the one Mr. Kalbfus had said he'd do right away, on the tacit agreement that I wouldn't tell the police the old man was there. A policeman was standing there, too, close to him.

Colonel Primrose spoke, crisp and hard: "Who found him?"

"This fellow. . . . What's your name, mister?"

"My name's Digges. . . . I found him, colonel. Just the way you see him."

"Clear out, all of you," Colonel Primrose said. . . . "You stay, Digges. . . . When's Lamb coming?"

"He's on his way, sir."

"Keep all this place clean. And put in a call to my place for Sergeant Buck."

That was unnecessary. The top of the garbage can came flying out of the passage, a soggy orange peel spotted with coffee grounds rolled at my feet. Sergeant Buck came into the yard in a hurry.

"I'll be a son of a——"

He came to an abrupt halt, vocally and physically. As he saw me—which is always a pleasure to both of us—he turned a sort of dark black with a yellow ocher and light red mixed in.

"Excuse me, ma'am." He got those words out of the corner of his mouth with difficulty, and strode into the shed. Inside he came to a sort of attention. "Something off color here, sir?"

Colonel Primrose, standing in front of Magnussen's pathetic body, moved aside a little.

Sergeant Buck took a step forward. "Nice work, sir," he said. I think he meant that Colonel Primrose was already on the job.

A young reporter edged over to me. "You're with the colonel, aren't you?"

I nodded.

"That's the old guy they've been hunting?"

I nodded again.

He shook his head. "That's bad, you know. If he'd sat tight he'd probably have got away with it. I mean the other one."

"What are you talking about?" I demanded.

"Lady, you wouldn't fool me, would you?" he asked reproachfully. "I mean Hilyard. The colonel and Lamb both know it too. They've been trying to keep it out of the papers, and keep this guy out of jail as long as they can. Pressure, lady. He knows more about the promethium business than anybody in the country."

"You may know," I said.

"They put Digges through the line-up and that oysterman picked him—like that. It was one of those old grudges. You know—they die, but nobody buries 'em."

I could feel my heart beginning to sink a little.

"I was over on Volta Place when this call came in," he said. "I dashed over with the cops. He was right here with that cop by him. He said he came in and found the old guy like that. Couldn't have been dead five minutes even then."

"I don't see, in that case, why he didn't just walk out," I said.

"Head of the class for you, lady. That's just what he was going to do, and he ran smack into the frontispiece of the law, coming in to check a rumor that an old guy looking like the one they'd been hunting for was staying here at night."

"I don't believe it," I answered.

"Okay. The cop does, and that's plenty."

The smell of the yard and the garbage—or something—was making me sick and my knees unsteady. The big policeman by me took hold of my arm.

"Here's a box you can sit on, lady," he said.

I was still sitting there, thinking I must look even worse than I thought, when Captain Lamb and Colonel Primrose came out of the shed. They talked quietly by the door for a few minutes. Then Colonel Primrose came over to me.

"Don't do this unless you feel up to it," he said. "It would help if you could identify this man as the one you saw on Prospect Street. I'd rather not call in any of the Hilyards just now. Can you?"

I hesitated. It wasn't that I couldn't do it. I had a primitive upsurge of sheer brutality for an instant. I wanted Mrs. Hilyard to be confronted with this thing. It was her fault even more than it was mine. I didn't see why she should be allowed to escape everything.

"There's a reason," he said, "or I wouldn't ask you."

I got up.

"Thank you, my dear. As soon as the photographers are through."

We waited a few moments. It seemed endless. The coroner had come, and a battery of technicians of all kinds. I could hear the subdued siren of the ambulance out on Wisconsin Avenue.

I went into the shed with Colonel Primrose. They had partly covered his head and were raising him to a cleared place on Mr. Kalbfus' worktable. As they moved him, something that had been held there by the weight of his body rolled off the bench. We all stood there staring at it for an instant until Sergeant Buck bent down, picked it up carefully and handed it to the colonel.

It was a thick roll of bills secured by a rubber band. I could see the denomination of the outside one; it was a fifty. Colonel Primrose held them for a moment, his black eyes snapping, and handed them to Captain Lamb. He took the band off gingerly and peeled the bills off one by one. There were twenty of them, all fifties, and all except the outside two as crisp and fresh as the day they'd come from the Bureau of Engraving on Fourteenth Street.

"One thousand dollars," Captain Lamb said. "Beggar, my foot! The old psalm-singing devil!" He turned to Colonel Primrose. "Blackmail?"

I looked down at the dead face on the table. It was as calm as a summer's dawn. There was a kind of quiet strength in it, but no guile or cunning, nor any fear or dread of God's great judgment seat.

"I don't believe it," Bowen Digges said shortly, and I heard my own voice say, "I don't either."

The men looked from one of us to the other without comment.

"You've seen this man before, Mrs. Latham?" Captain Lamb asked.

I nodded.

I'd seen him. It was a face that no one could ever forget.

"Where?"

"On Prospect Street, last Monday between five and six o'clock. He crossed the avenue to speak to Mr. Hilyard. Mr. Hilyard drove away, leaving him standing in the street. I also——"

Colonel Primrose's hand closed on my arm. I stopped short.

"What were you going to say, Mrs. Latham?"

"I started to say I saw him a little later on Thirty-third Street," I went on, with half the truth. "He was waiting to cross the street, I thought. But he turned and went back along Prospect Street toward Thirty-seventh."

I looked again at the table. It's strange, but now that all sign of violence was gone, there was nothing terrible, only something deeply moving, about the man lying there. His face was like the face of the spirit in the Blake drawing of the Death of the Good Old Man. I suppose it was because no one there felt any personal bereavement; or possibly in a world where there is no peace, the profundity of the peace and dignity he had achieved seemed a kind of miracle.

Sergeant Buck bent down again, picked up the Bible lying on the floor, keeping it open as it had fallen, and looked at the page the old man had been reading. Then, to my surprise, as I hadn't really thought he could do it, he read, very slowly and after clearing that iron throat of his with a resounding crash:

" 'I have seen the wicked in great power, and spreading himself like a green bay tree.

" 'Yet he passed away, and, lo, he was not; yea, I sought him, but he could not be found.' "

There was a little silence.

"He had it marked there," Buck said.

Colonel Primrose took the Bible from the sergeant's hands and stood looking down at it for a long time before he handed it to a detective and got on with his job.

How he got Bowen Digges off—I mean even in the most temporary way—I wouldn't know. They took down his story. It was the way the reporter had given it to me; except that he only said he'd heard Magnussen was staying there and wanted to see him. I thought Colonel Primrose started to ask something at that point, and stopped. As far as I knew, it was a straightforward story, beginning with seeing Magnussen and not recognizing him on the wharf. When he got to Mr. Kalbfus' shop, Magnussen was lying just as they found him.

When he had finished his account, Colonel Primrose and Captain Lamb had a long and earnest conversation and Bowen was handed over as the colonel's personal responsibility. And I assumed, with a lifting of my heart, that Colonel Primrose didn't think Bowen had killed either Lawrason Hilyard or the old man. If he had thought so he'd never have sent him home with me, I hoped. I didn't know at the time that he sent Sergeant Buck along behind us. If I had known it I'd have assumed he thought Bowen and I were in a conspiracy, both tarred with the same bloody brush.

"I'll be along shortly," he said.

I don't think Bowen and I said ten words on the way home, or before dinner, or during it, or after. He had plenty to think about, heaven knew, and so did I. He sat by the fire with Sheila curled up at his feet. He didn't smoke and he wouldn't drink. He just sat staring into the fire. At dinner he did eat, first because Lilac told him to, and after that because he was hungry. He was sitting by the fire again when Colonel Primrose came in. It was nearly nine o'clock.

Colonel Primrose came over to the fire. "Did either you or the patrolman look around that place at all?" he asked shortly.

Bowen shook his head. "I dashed out to put in a call, and met him head on in the passage. I wanted to stay, but he hauled me along to the call box."

"Someone was standing behind the tree in the back yard," Colonel Primrose said. "Probably when you and that dumb ox were there. He tracked garbage back, and there's plenty of evidence of uneasy waiting."

"Oh, God!" Bowen said. "If I'd looked around——"

Colonel Primrose nodded. "It's not really important," he said urbanely, "but you might have been killed too. The important thing——" He stopped for a moment. "I'd like to talk to Mrs. Latham. . . . Can Digges go upstairs, or somewhere?"

"The boys' sitting room in front," I said. "Right at the end of the hall. There's a radio and a lot of books."

Bowen got up without a word.

"Just one question first. What did you want to see Magnussen about?"

I'd got, it seemed to me, so I could tell when Mr. Digges was, in effect, saying, "That's my business too." He didn't exactly now. He stopped, hesitated, and said, "He was an old acquaintance. I used to be his helper at the plant."

"Thank you," Colonel Primrose said.

When Bowen had gone, he came over and sat down by me.

"Begin at the beginning, Mrs. Latham," he said seriously. "Don't leave anything out. If I can't prove something I only guess at now, Digges goes to jail at midnight. I'll turn him over. Unless——" He drew a deep breath. "I don't think the boy's guilty, of course. The evidence convicts him—and there's more of it than you know. But the pattern is too——" He stopped again.

"There's more of it than you know," I said. "Carey Eaton saw him pick up Mr. Hilyard's gun and put it in his pocket."

"So Eaton told me this noon—with great reluctance."

"Was that what you meant in your note, about its being more serious?"

He nodded. "Partly. That isn't all. I know, officially, that it was Digges' hat your setter found on the canal bank. I can't keep it to myself much longer."

I stared at him, open-mouthed.

"How . . . do you know it?" I managed to say. "Who told you?"

"Diane," he said calmly.

"Diane Hilyard?"

He nodded. "Yes. Diane Hilyard."

18

"I DON'T BELIEVE IT," I SAID. "I simply can't. It just doesn't make any possible kind of sense."

"It makes a great deal," he said. "If only I could manage to get you to be indiscreet at the right time instead of the wrong time."

I looked at him blankly. "Me?" I asked. Then I began to understand him a little. "You don't think it would have made any difference if I hadn't told Bowen——"

I was horribly distressed.

"Not to Magnussen," he said. "I'm not certain it would have made any difference to him if you'd got hold of me this morning. It would have made a difference to Digges. But that's not what I meant."

"What did you mean?"

He chuckled a little at the look on my face.

"Diane Hilyard," he said, very seriously, "was doing an extraordinarily intelligent thing."

"Intelligent?"

He nodded. "The bravest and most intelligent thing she could have done, Mrs. Latham."

I just sat there staring at him.

"Diane jumped to a probably right conclusion," he said. "Intuitively, not rationally. Then she proceeded to act on it as a rational person. And if you'd told her I suspected the two of you of concealing that hat, and that I was waiting for developments, it would have been damned disloyal of you and I'd never have dared trust you again." He smiled again. "But if you had, it would certainly have saved the immediate situation."

"This is too paradoxical, or something, for me," I said wearily. "You'll just have to use words of one syllable."

"There was a sisterly row, in the first place. Diane still balked at the suicide theory. Her sister, Mrs. Eaton, in a final devastating attempt to bring her around, told her that Carey Eaton had seen Digges put the gun in his pocket. Also that he'd been keeping it to himself because he wanted to spare her."

"I heard about that," I said.

"Well, it didn't sound plausible to Diane. And she came—suddenly, I gather—to a terrible conclusion— that Digges was being made the victim of a gigantic fraud, either to save someone else or deliberately destroy him. 'Framed' is the technical word. And she decided that every shred of evidence that had been planted against him—her conclusion being true—ought to be exposed, so the truth could come out. I think it took great courage to come to that decision."

"I do, too," I said slowly. "Both on account of Bowen Digges and of her family."

He didn't say anything.

"But how horrible!" I said.

"I know. There are people like that. Well, that's how it happened. I think, by the way, that Diane's mistaken about the primary motive here. Somebody wanted to get rid of Hilyard in the worst possible way—for what reason I have only a general idea. Magnussen might possibly have told us."

He stopped for a moment, looking at me. "I'm not sure he didn't tell us. Anyway, if it could be passed off as suicide, fine. If not, let Digges take the rap. And he would have, if it hadn't just happened that I'd been interested in Hilyard already." He stopped again, looking at me seriously. "I want you to report, my dear. Let me do the interpreting. I don't want to hear what you think, I want to hear what you know. And don't forget that Digges is a complicated human being. And don't leave anything out."

I reported, beginning at the beginning. I even got out Agnes Philips' letter again and gave it to him. I told him about the quarrel Mr. and Mrs. Hilyard were having when I went into their house Monday evening, and about her rapping on the window when Magnussen was crossing the street toward Mr. Hilyard's car. It was all terribly clear. The conversations I'd had with them or had heard them having, the graphic scenes— the Eatons stopping when my radio was blaring out that congressional attack on the promethium setup; Mrs. Hilyard, black-shrouded, waiting for Magnussen on

the terrace, her collapse at lunch on the Samarkand—
were acutely vivid in my mind.

I kept seeing Mrs. Hilyard's hands too; and although telling about that seemed a feline kind of comment to make about another woman, I made it. My
conversations with her, and with Diane and Bowen,
Carey Eaton and Joan and Bartlett Folger, Mr. Kalbfus and Lilac, I could quote almost word for word. I
told him about Diane's typewriter and the letter, and
the business of atonement as Bartlett Folger had told
it to me. It seemed trivial to mention the lock on the
tilt-top table that Magnussen had helped Mr. Kalbfus
with, but I did. I didn't leave anything out that I'd
seen or heard.

Stanley Woland I barely brought in at all, except as
Diane had talked about him. Poor Stanley seemed to
have dropped down a drain, really. Anyway, he had no
motive at all for framing Bowen Digges, even if he had
one for killing Lawrason Hilyard; and he certainly
wouldn't have risked exposing himself to the public eye
by going to Mr. Kalbfus' to crush the old man's head
in. In fact, he was the only person in the crowd that
I could give a perfectly clean bill of health to. Joan
Eaton no doubt was well pleased that her husband had
been at home after all, with an iron-clad and incon-
trovertible alibi, but it was Stanley who was really
lucky. It seemed amusing, when nothing else had a
glimmer of amusement in it, that what Stanley would
regard as the greatest conceivable misfortune should be
an extraordinary stroke of fool's luck.

"I'm afraid none of it's much help," I said.

I looked at the clock. In an hour and a quarter Bowen Digges would be turned over to Captain Lamb, and the newspapers would start pouring out enough ink to blacken him for the rest of his life, even if by a miracle he escaped the final penalty.

"Did you ever talk to Ira Colton?" Colonel Primrose asked, after a minute.

He seemed to come back from a long voyage into space. So did Ira Colton. I'd been so involved with emotional and immediate factors and people that I'd pretty much forgotten him.

"I never talked to him," I said. "I saw him, and I heard about his visit with that lawyer, Duncan Scott, to the Hilyards' Tuesday night."

"What did you hear?"

"I'd forgotten that. He broke a chair there, Boston said. I guess he was pretty mad. Scott seems to have taken it better, but lawyers usually can take their clients' losses with fortitude. And it seems to have been the two of them who saw Bowen pick up the gun. They wouldn't have any connection with Magnussen, would they?"

Colonel Primrose looked around at me for a brief instant. Then he got to his feet abruptly. He didn't leap up as Bowen Digges had done, but the movement had the same kind of sudden recognition. He went over to the telephone and dialed a number. I watched him blankly.

"Primrose speaking; Captain Lamb, please," he said.

He waited. "Hello, Lamb. I want twenty-four hours more. I know who did it. . . . Yes, I tell you I do. . . . Yes, I've got to have it. Send a man out to the Randolph-Lee and have him take Ira Colton and Duncan Scott out to Gallinger. Don't tell them why they're going. I want them to see Magnussen's body, and I want to be there when they do it. I'll be along in half an hour. . . . What? . . . Yes, I know they were in the Randolph-Lee bar at eleven thirty-five. . . ."

He listened. Captain Lamb's voice was harsh and excited.

"I know all that," Colonel Primrose said patiently. "I've told you from the beginning that this had a defense angle. And one thing more: Have them bring that skiff in—the one they used to carry Hilyard's body across the canal. I want to see it tonight." He put the phone down.

"What in the world is it?" I demanded. To say that I was in a complete, bewildering fog isn't enough. "What have I just said?"

He chuckled suddenly. "You've just said who murdered Lawrason Hilyard. I'm very grateful to you, my dear. I'll see you tomorrow. Good night. I'll take Digges with me."

"And I can't come?"

"You can't come. You stay right here, and don't go out till I say you can. You're the custodian of the hat. Take your job seriously."

I sat there trying to make a little intelligible sense

out of it. The whole thing, as far as I was concerned, had tumbled apart like a deck of cards. Unconsciously, or rather subconsciously, I'd worked up half a dozen cases against the Hilyards; chiefly, I suppose, because of their suicide pact and their "shielding" of Bowen Digges and Mrs. Hilyard's strange carryings-on with the dead man, Magnussen. That, I still couldn't understand. Why should she have made denial after denial that she knew him, when she not only did know him but knew where he could be found? And what did the thousand dollars that rolled from under his body on Mr. Kalbfus' bench mean except that somebody—if not Mrs. Hilyard definitely—had given it to him in payment for something?

Then something came into my mind like a flash of light in the dark. Mrs. Hilyard had given it to him, perhaps, for his mission, expecting that he'd go away, wanting him to go, for some reason not known to me. That would explain how he could be persuaded to take the money, and also why she collapsed at lunch on the Samarkand when Bartlett Folger said he had just seen him on the wharf.

But it left so much unexplained: Why he'd come, in the first place. What he'd been doing. Why they wanted him out of the way. It seemed always to come back to "they"—the triumvirate of Mrs. Hilyard, her daughter Joan, her son-in-law Carey Eaton. Except, I thought suddenly, that it was Diane Hilyard who had prevented Bartlett Folger from calling the police and having the old man arrested. He might still be alive if she hadn't pulled out that telephone connection. She and I might be as responsible for his death as the person who murdered him.

I gave it all up, reached over to the end of the sofa and picked up the paper. I hadn't had a chance to read much of it before Bowen came. His face looked up at me from the page, clean-cut and straightforward. I read the heavy newsprint again. If Carey Eaton should manage to get his place——

The spectacle of Sergeant Buck reading the marked passage in the old man's Bible flashed back into my mind. I tried to remember how it went, and finally got up and looked it up in the Psalms.

"I have seen the wicked in great power, and spreading himself like a green bay tree.

"Yet he passed away, and, lo, he was not; yea, I sought him, but he could not be found."

I tried desperately to think what it was in there that had kept Colonel Primrose staring down at it so long. Magnussen had sought Lawrason Hilyard, and Hilyard could not be found—in a sense, I supposed. He had also passed away, and he was not. But that didn't seem very helpful, somehow.

19

I TOOK THE NEWSPAPER UP AGAIN and glanced down the page. Near the bottom was an item I hadn't noticed. It said, DEMOCRACY AT WORK. Under it was SMALL BUSINESSMAN INTERVIEWS OPM HEADS. It said:

The story of how a small businessman made himself heard was revealed today. Mr. Ira B. Colton, president and manager of the Colton Novelty Company, proposed Carey Eaton, now with the Board of Economic Warfare, to succeed his late father-in-law, Lawrason Hilyard, as promethium chief. The police are still investigating Mr. Hilyard's alleged suicide. Colton claimed that a young man actively connected with the industry was urgently needed to head the promethium division of OPM.

Asked if he opposed the appointment of Bowen Digges, present acting head, Colton said he had nothing against Digges personally, and that he was undoubtedly an able metallurgist. The crying need at the present moment, however, was for a man who knows the industrial end of the problem confronting the nation in times like these. His attempts to negotiate with both Hilyard and Digges, Colton stated, had been marked with shilly-shallying and delay, of a sort that would ruin thousands of small businesses unless a change of policy and personnel was effected at once. He told reporters the men he talked with at OPM were interested in his suggestion.

Colton spoke highly of Eaton as a hard-boiled, two-fisted businessman who knows promethium from the practical angle.

Well, I thought.

Until Sheila looked up and thumped her tail on the floor, I hadn't realized I'd spoken aloud. She got up, started over to me and stopped, pricking up her ears and looking out into the hall. I sat up, listening. The house was silent. She growled and gave a sharp little bark. I heard a fumbling noise at the door, and the bell rang.

I looked at the clock. It was twenty minutes past eleven. For a moment I thought I wouldn't answer, and then I thought it might be Diane, or Bowen coming back. I went out into the hall, turned on the ceiling light and opened the door. Then I took a step backward from sheer surprise. It was Mr. Kalbfus.

He looked as yellow as saffron and incredibly old and forlorn, standing there nervously, his hat in his hands, his bald egg of a head glistening under the light.

"I'm sorry to bother you this time of night, Mrs. Latham," he began.

"It's quite all right," I said. "Come in, won't you?"

He followed me into the sitting room and stood in the middle of the floor, moving his hat around in his hands.

"Sit down, Mr. Kalbfus," I said. "I'll get you a bottle of beer."

He shook his head, but I went downstairs to the kitchen to get it anyway. Lilac's door was closed. I could hear her snoring peacefully, and I didn't turn on the light, for fear she'd wake and come grumbling out, wanting to know what I was doing in her kitchen. I made my way quietly across to the icebox, started to open it and stopped, my heart suddenly a frozen lump in my throat. There was someone in the area outside the kitchen door. A dark shadow had moved silently across the window toward the recess under the front doorsteps. I could hear something scrape softly across the iron garbage can and stop there.

My first impulse was to streak like a rabbit back up the stairs and call the police. My second and more considered one was to find out who was out there before he got away. I forced myself to open the icebox quietly, not looking toward the window, and get out the bottle of beer. I took a glass out of the cupboard, started toward the stairs, turned and tiptoed over to the door and put the bottle and glass on the drainboard.

If I could get the latch chain down without any noise,

I could turn the lock and switch on the light as I opened the door. I was trying to remember whether the screen door was still up or not when I heard a sound on the other side. A milk bottle fell over and rolled on the concrete floor. Then I could hear footsteps, and I ran around to the window.

A man's legs were visible dashing up the steps. He wore an overcoat with the collar turned up, and his head was down so that I couldn't see his face; but as he got to the top and turned left, his coat caught on the end of the iron guardrail.

He turned back and jerked it off, his head still down, and then sprinted on. But it was too late. I'd seen the end of his nose and his cheekbone and the side of his jaw.

I stood there for a while quite breathless, my heart not in my throat any more—in fact, not anywhere that I could feel it beating.

I must have stood there a very long time. It was so stupefying, someway. What possible reason had Stanley Woland to be lurking in my areaway at half past eleven at night?

20

WHEN I WAS ABLE TO THINK COLLECTEDLY, my reaction was just plain anger. I was furious. It was a plain violent uprush of adrenalin. The idea of being afraid of Stanley Woland would never, under any circumstances, have occurred to me. I picked up the bottle and glass and marched upstairs, so mad that I could have burst. That all vanished, however, when I saw poor Mr. Kalbfus sitting gingerly on the edge of the chair by the fire, old and wan and destroyed, with Sheila, her head between his knees, looking up at him as if she'd lost her last friend too.

They both brightened up as I came in.

"They didn't keep me in jail," Mr. Kalbfus said.

"I should hope not," I answered warmly.

I put the glass and the beer on the table by him. He poured it out slowly against the side of the glass.

"I kept trying to tell them, but they don't believe me," he said. "So I gave up. Maybe you can tell Colonel Primrose. My father did work for his mother in the old shop."

That was a little surprising. I'd never thought of Colonel Primrose as having a mother. Sergeant Buck, indeed, had told somebody that the Primrose house on

197

P Street had descended from father to son through seven generations of John Primroses, all officers and all bachelors.

"What won't they listen to?" I asked.

"About the old fellow. About the money."

Mr. Kalbfus wiped his mouth with the back of his hand and looked at me anxiously.

"He had it all the time. Nobody paid it to him. He had it in a canvas bag, tied hanging under his arm. I didn't ever see it; I just saw the bag and the way he was so careful about it. But they won't believe me. They said somebody would have stolen it. I think he'd been saving it up for something. For a long time."

I tried hard to readjust my theory about Mrs. Hilyard.

"He never said anything about himself, or where he was from, or anything?" I asked.

Mr. Kalbfus shook his head.

"What about that chair—the one you were doing this morning?"

"The lady came and got it this evening."

"Was he there when she came?"

Mr. Kalbfus nodded. "That's the first I really thought he was crazy. When she walked in, he just put down a file he was using and stood looking at her like it was Judgment Day sure enough. I took the chair out to her car for her. I said, 'I've never seen him act like that before.' She said she didn't notice anything out of the way, so I didn't say anything else. Maybe I just imagined it."

I didn't say anything.

"It's too bad," Mr. Kalbfus went on. "It just takes the heart out of you. I just can't think about anything, seeing him there. The people in the front called me and told me the police were back there. I thought maybe they figured he didn't have any right to be there, so I hurried over to tell them he was all right. He was such a nice harmless old fellow. I'd swear he never got that money dishonestly."

It was after twelve when he left. I bolted the door and went upstairs. I might have been Macbeth, sleep had so effectively deserted me. It was after one when I turned on the light, reached for the phone and dialed Colonel Primrose's number. I don't know whether he ever sleeps; he always sounds perfectly wide-awake and the phone never rings but once.

"It's Grace Latham, colonel," I said. "I've got two things to tell you. Mr. Kalbfus came. He says Magnussen already had that money, and that he looked like Judgment Day sure enough when Mrs. Hilyard came for her chair."

"What's the second?" he said. He sounded exactly as if humoring a spoiled but favorite child.

"The second is that I had a nocturnal prowler kicking over my milk bottles in the area."

I thought that would surprise him, but I could hear him chuckling exasperatingly.

"Dear, dear," he said. "I gather you recognized Stanley, or you wouldn't be so grim about it."

"Did you know about Mr. Kalbfus too?"

"Of course. You didn't think I'd trust you not to go prowling around and probably getting yourself murdered, did you?"

I couldn't think of an answer to that.

"Furthermore, I don't want anything to happen to Digges' hat."

"I see, now," I said.

"He's here with me, by the way. Lamb's given us rope enough to last till midnight."

"What about Ira B. Colton?"

"Magnussen worked for him for about four years. He was laid off six weeks ago when the promethium reserves ran out. Colton says he was a fine mechanic and crazy as a bedbug. He's cut up about it, now he thinks he can get some promethium."

"Can he?" I was surprised at that.

"He seems to think so. I don't know why. Now you go to sleep. Don't be alarmed if you hear anyone. You're safe."

"I hope," I said. "I'd rather have Stanley here than Sergeant Buck, if it's all the same to you."

"Well, it's not. Good night, my dear."

I was waked up by the phone at ten minutes to eight. I waited for the buzzer to sound, which would indicate that Lilac regarded the call as important enough for me to answer before she brought my breakfast. It did sound, but after so long a time that I knew she'd decided only after grave doubts. And when I answered, I don't think, on the whole, that I could have been more surprised. It was Stanley himself, and as I knew—all other things apart—that he prided himself on never being up until ten or eleven, it was obvious that something was gravely wrong.

"Grace, have you seen the papers?" he demanded quickly.

"I just woke up," I said. "Why?"

"Because I've got to see you, or somebody, right away."

"Then why didn't you ring the doorbell last night, instead of prowling around the area?" I asked.

The silence at the other end was so lengthy that I thought he'd rung off. But he hadn't.

"I don't know what you're talking about," he said. "I haven't left the house for days."

"It's nights I'm talking about, darling," I said.

He let it go. "I've got to see you right away. It's important. Will you come over? Please, Grace. I can't go out."

"All right," I said. "As soon as I can. Is it all right to bring Colonel Primrose?"

He hesitated. "If you want to. I didn't know you were so old-fashioned."

"Then I'll bring Diane instead," I said. I put the phone down before he could answer.

The papers were grim enough, heaven knows, even without the Hilyard case or the murder of the old man named Magnussen. I looked hurriedly down the left-hand column. It was devoted to both of them, as if the connection was already firmly and publicly established. Bowen's name was mentioned openly for the first time, though only in connection with his discovery of Magnussen's body.

It was what they called NEW DEVELOPMENTS IN OPM DEATH that startled me.

It was authoritatively disclosed at headquarters late last night that the police are in possession of two articles of clothing presumed to have been worn by a man closely connected with the dead dollar-a-year OPM metal magnate. The police refused to give out his name at this time. He is known to have been questioned several times, and is under surveillance. Stains on the clothing alleged to have been worn by him on the night before the millionaire industrialist's body was found in the C. & O. Canal have been examined. It was learned today that tests showed the stains to be blood, and that they are what is known in blood analysis as Type 2. Tests also revealed that the blood of the dead promethium king was Type 2.

The hat missing since the police arrived at the death scene on the canal, and alleged to have been thrown away by the daughter of the dead man, has also been recovered.

My heart sank to the pit of my stomach. But the most startling item followed:

The police declined to reveal its whereabouts, and

refused any comment, other than to confirm a rumor that reporters dug up from a servant of one of the individuals concerned.

I put the paper down.

"Lilac!" I said sharply. "Come here at once."

She was just starting down the stairs, and she came back, blinking at me in apprehension.

"Yes, Miss Grace."

"Lilac, did you tell anyone I had a man's hat in this house?" I demanded.

"You mean that ol' hat in th' chest out there in th' hall under my tablecloth?"

"Yes."

" 'Deed, Miss Grace, Ah ain' tol' nobody. 'Cept the sergeant. He ain' nobody. He's home folks."

"Did you tell Boston?"

" 'Deed Ah ain' tol' Boston nothin'," she said belligerently. "He say they askin' roun' over there did he see a hat. Ah said, if anybody come roun' here askin' for a hat, Ah throw the dishwater in their faces."

It wouldn't, I thought, need a very bright reporter to see through that.

"Take the tray," I said, "and hand me my slippers and robe."

I got out of bed and put them on and got the key out of my dressing-table drawer. She followed me out into the hall to the chest-on-chest. I unlocked the drawer and picked up the tablecloth.

Bowen's hat was gone.

I just stood there for a moment. Then I said, "Lilac, what day did Boston tell you about their asking for the hat?"

"Day before yes'day," she answered. "Tha's Thursday, ain' it?"

I went back to my room and dialed Colonel Primrose again. Lilac came back in.

"Miss Grace," she said, "Ah forgot to tell you. It was th' sergeant took that hat. He said you might fo'get an' throw it in the fire. He took it Wednesday night when you was out."

I could feel the blood seeping up into my face. I put down the phone and drew a long deep breath.

"An' he say," Lilac went on, "that when anybody come roun' askin' 'bout that hat, Ah was to make pretense it was here, but Ah wasn' sayin' it is or it ain'. Now you drink you' coffee an' cover up. You'll freeze to death. Ol' Jack Fros' out here this mornin'."

I think I could have borne all that, difficult as it was, but I wasn't prepared for the final straw. When I dressed and went downstairs, Sergeant Buck was down in the kitchen, eating breakfast enough to feed the German people for the Nazi duration. And Bowen's hat was lying on my living-room table.

21

THERE WERE CARS PARKED ALL ALONG
Stanley's side of Adams Place, so that I had to park
quite a ways down the block. I got out and started
along, stopped and took a second look ahead of me. A
woman was just crossing the sidewalk in front of his
house to her car. I thought at first it was Mrs. Hilyard. Then I realized that, oddly enough, it really was
Mrs. Hilyard, and that she was coming from Stanley's.
It seemed reasonable enough for me to be surprised
at it, after all the elaborate camouflage of his staying
in and creeping out after dark to keep people from seeing that somebody had violently assaulted him. It was
even more surprising to think that Mrs. Hilyard apparently still had the idea that Diane was going to
marry him.

I went on slowly until she pulled out and turned the
corner at the end of the block. Stanley's Filipino house-
man opened the door tentatively and squinted through
the crack. He recognized me instantly, took the chain
down and opened the door with smiles and bows; I suppose relieved that I hadn't brought an Army officer
along this time.

Stanley was not only down, he was dressed.

"I thought you weren't receiving," I said. I put my coat over the back of the sofa. It must have been the only time in Stanley's life that he hadn't bounded to help a woman off with her wrap.

"I'm not," he said.

"I thought I saw Mrs. Hilyard just leaving."

He gave me a jittery glance. "She didn't come in; she just brought some flowers. There they are over on the table. Good Lord, can't a——"

"Oh, hush," I said wearily. "I don't care if the Empress of Japan calls on you, darling. What is it you want?"

He went the rest of the way to the window and came back. Just as he'd got to the other sofa facing me the telephone rang.

He jumped as if a firecracker had gone off in church. The phone was right by me, and he must have thought I was going to answer it, because he shot around and picked it up before the little brass *objets* on the shelf had quit tingling.

"Hello."

I was so close that I could hear the voice at the other end.

"Hello, Stanley. John Primrose speaking. I believe Mrs. Latham is there. I'd like to speak to her, please. How are you, by the way?"

Stanley looked rather taken aback. "Yes, she's here. She's just come. I'm all right, thanks."

I took the phone quickly, not imagining what could

have happened. Or how he knew where I was, for that matter.

"Hello."

"Hello," he said placidly. "That's all I wanted to say, really. Just keeping track of you, that's all."

"You mean that's the only reason you called?" I demanded. "In that case, let me tell you something. I nearly fired my cook this morning, before I discovered your perfidy about the hat. You can just take it out of my house right away."

There was a sort of shocked silence at the other end of the line. I realized with complete horror that I shouldn't have said it. Stanley would probably tell Mrs. Hilyard the minute I left the house.

"And if Stanley mentions it, I'll phone every newspaper in town about his black eye," I added.

Colonel Primrose chuckled. "I'll see you shortly."

I put the phone down. Stanley was opening a fresh pack of cigarettes.

"Does he call up everywhere you go?" he asked. "Why don't you marry him and be done with it?"

"Because he never asked me in the second place," I said. "And you know the first place, darling?"

"I know it's none of my business, but——"

"Look, Stanley," I said patiently. "If that's what you woke me up at daybreak and got me over here to talk about, I'm going back right now."

"It's not. I want to talk to you about this fellow Digges."

"Then go ahead. And quit roaming around! Can't you sit down and quit being so jittery?"

"You'd be jittery too. You don't seem to realize what all this means to me!"

He sat down opposite me. "This is the point," he said. "I know Diane isn't going to marry me now, un-less—— Oh, well, we'll skip that. But this Digges. They're going to arrest him for the murder of Hilyard."

"Really?" I said. "How did you know?"

"Because he's the chap whose clothes they're talking about in the morning paper."

"It doesn't say so. How did you know?"

"Because it's my blood on his clothes!" He almost screamed it.

"Oh," I said.

"It was my nose!" he cried. "He hit me! Twice, three times—I don't know! He knocked me down! Then he picked me up—and that's when he got the blood on him! My nose was like a fountain!"

"Then he didn't kill Mr. Hilyard," I remarked. "Stanley! You're wonderful!"

"But wait, Grace! You don't understand. That doesn't prove anything! All it proves is about the blood. It was after Mr. Hilyard was killed that it hap-pened. It was twelve o'clock. Here! Here in my own house! Right upstairs!"

"Do you mean he came here deliberately and at-tacked you?" I demanded.

"Yes! Oh, yes!"

"But why?"

"So I couldn't go out! So I couldn't marry Diane!"
He was almost sobbing. "She didn't have a headache.
That isn't why we came back early from the ball. She
was angry at him. She'd just seen him the night before.
She thought he was probably married to the girl he was
with. She was unhappy—so unhappy! And so angry!
I persuaded her to run away with me and get married
right away. I was eloquent and comforting. We had to
come home and change. I took her home. Digges was
there with her father and that Eaton person. She
marched in and told them, the three of them, to their
faces, what she was going to do. Oh, it was so foolish!"

He put his battered face down in his hands, shaking
with remembered anguish. I didn't for a minute doubt
that it was very genuine.

"Her father was in a rage. He ordered her upstairs.
She went like a child. He went and locked her door—
like a father in the old country. When he came back,
he talked to me like a madman. I went out. Diane threw
me down a piece of paper, outside. It said to come at
half past twelve; she'd get out." His head went down
again. "But I must have dropped it! This Digges knew!
He came at twelve. I was getting ready to go. She was
waiting. He came here. He broke the chain off the
door! He came upstairs! He stood in my door, and he
said, 'This hurts me worse than it does you, you louse!'
He called me a louse!"

"You've been called that before, Stanley," I said.

"But not the same!" he groaned. "He said, 'I'm

going to fix that mug of yours so she can't marry you tonight or next week. When she's had time to think about it, it's her business.' And then——"

"Oh, don't go on," I said. "I can guess the rest of it."

He was really sobbing now, with pain and humiliation and futile, frustrated rage.

"Why don't you sue him?" I asked.

His head shot up. "No! That's what I'm telling you, Grace! The publicity! Don't you see? That's the point! Unless the police understand it's not Hilyard's blood before the trial—don't you see? He'll keep quiet as long as he can—not for me, for Diane—but when he sees the noose he'll tell. And then——" His hands spread wide in an eloquent gesture. "I will be laughed at everywhere. All over the world. I cannot stand it!" He broke down again, his face in his hands, shaking convulsively.

"I can see that," I agreed. Then I thought of something. "Stanley, did you see him take Mr. Hilyard's gun?"

He nodded. "It was me he was going to kill," he said wretchedly. "I wish he had. I could have died easier than I can face my friends if this is known. He put the gun in his pocket and he said, 'If you marry Diane tonight, I'll blow your brains out.' "

"So that was it. What did you say? Didn't you get a word in at all?"

He shook his head. "Not then. When he came here

I was angry too. I laughed at him. I said, 'What right have you to talk? They paid you twenty-five hundred dollars to get out of town so you couldn't marry her. You accepted. You have no right to speak now!' Oh, that was such a mistake! That was what Eaton told me; I didn't know it was a lie."

"You do now, I guess," I said. "It was a mistake in any case. What do you want me to do?"

"Make Colonel Primrose understand!" He was almost on his knees. "You must do it, Grace! No one else can do it for me! I would die of shame!"

"You still haven't told me what you were prowling around my garbage cans for last night," I said.

"I can't go out in the daytime, Grace. A man came just as I got there. I had to wait. You see, don't you?"

"Yes, I see," I said. I reached for the phone and dialed Colonel Primrose's number.

"Look, colonel," I said. "I've got some information that will interest you. Can you meet me at my house pretty soon? You might bring Bowen if he's still with you."

22

THEY WERE GOING IN THE DOOR JUST AS I GOT home. Colonel Primrose apparently hadn't told Bowen where I'd been. He couldn't have looked as unconcerned as he did, holding the door for me. He didn't look very unconcerned a moment later as he followed me and the colonel into my living room. And it wasn't the sight of his hat, still lying on the table, because he didn't even see that. It was Diane Hilyard, on the ottoman in front of the fire.

She got up quickly. "I'd better go," she said. She reached for her coat. "I didn't know you were busy."

"No. I think you'd better stay," Colonel Primrose said urbanely. "It's time you two were getting straightened out a little. . . . This is your hat, isn't it, Digges?"

"I guess so," Bowen said. His voice was carefully controlled. "If it's got my name in it. I don't wear one often enough to tell it from anybody else's." He looked inside it and handed it back. "That's mine."

"When did you have it last?"

"Tuesday night when I left the Hilyards'. That's the last I remember."

"All right," Colonel Primrose said. "Sit down, you two."

"Colonel, I don't know," I said uneasily, "whether Diane's going to like——"

"It doesn't make a great deal of difference whether she likes it or not," he said calmly. "It's time she was hearing the truth, and it's time Digges was telling it. I'm sure she can take it, whatever it is."

She shot him a quick, radiant smile. "Thanks, colonel!" she said. She settled back into her chair with the dignity of a very young and very sweet goddess. Bowen reached for a cigarette and started to light it, getting a shade more like a thundercloud.

"Very well, then," I said. "Here goes, but don't blame me. Stanley doesn't want it to come out in court that the blood on Bowen's overcoat is his, because it will ruin his career."

The match in Bowen's fingers burned down until he dropped it.

"Look here, colonel," he began angrily.

"Sit down, Digges," Colonel Primrose said. "You've been a fool long enough. . . . Go on, Mrs. Latham."

I went on from there to the bitter end.

I could see Diane all the time. Her face was an extraordinary kaleidoscope of a dozen emotions, from distress to chagrin to quick amusement and all the way back again. And Bowen just sat glowering, sunk down in the corner of the sofa, his face a dull brick red, his eyes fixed on a point on the floor—midway between a couple of circles of hell.

Only at one point did anybody interrupt me. That

was when I got to the episode of Diane's marching in, as Stanley had described, and telling them all what she was going to do.

And it was Diane who interrupted. She got up quickly, her cheeks flaming scarlet.

"I'm sorry!" she cried passionately. "I didn't know what I was doing! I was—— Oh, I don't know why I was such a horrid pig!"

It was the only time that Bowen looked up, so far as I know. If he could have seen himself just then, he'd have known that not even the letter, even if she had written it, made any real difference to him.

"I'm going home," Diane whispered. "I can't bear it."

"In a minute or two," Colonel Primrose said.

She sat down, and didn't move again; nor did Bowen Digges, until I got to the gun. The movement then was a sort of deepened silence, and it lasted to the end.

For a moment nobody said anything. Diane sat with her hands folded in her lap, looking down at them, tears beading her long lashes.

"Well, let's hear about that gun, Digges," Colonel Primrose said patiently.

"I took it, all right. I guess I was going to kill him. And I would have if I'd had it, but I didn't."

"What happened to it?"

"Mr. Hilyard and I were there in the library. Woland had gone, and so had Eaton. Mr. Hilyard was so sore he couldn't stand still, but even then he had more sense than I had. He asked me to take a walk with him; he had to cool off, and he had something to tell me. I said okay. He called the dog, and then he said, 'You'd better give me that gun. No use having a weapon on you when you feel like using it.' He put it back in the drawer, and that's the last I saw of it."

"Go on," Colonel Primrose said.

"When we got outside I saw a crumpled piece of paper by the steps that wasn't there when I came in, and I picked it up. I didn't want to tell Mr. Hilyard, because I thought he'd make it unpleasant for her. He wanted to go down and walk on the towing path. We went down to Thirty-fourth and M in my car. A little ways along Prospect I saw Woland's car. I guessed he was waiting to go back, and said so. Mr. Hilyard said Diane was locked in, and she couldn't get out anyway unless Mrs. Hilyard let her out. He said if she did, and encouraged her to go with Woland, that would bring Diane to her senses quicker than anything else, because Mrs. Hilyard was a fool and Diane knew it."

Diane was still looking down, the spots on her cheeks hotter and darker.

"We walked about a mile. I was in a hurry by that time. It was half past eleven. We started back, but the spaniel wouldn't come. Mr. Hilyard might as well have whistled for the wind. I left him a couple of hundred yards from the bridge, still whistling. I was running, because I didn't want to be too late where I was going. And that's the last I saw of him, standing there on the towing path, whistling. He said for me to go on; he might be there an hour. Diane had never taught the dog to obey any better than she'd been taught herself."

He looked over at her and grinned in spite of himself; and she laughed a little, then put her handkerchief quickly up to her face. "Poor dad," she whispered.

Bowen moved unhappily.

"What was it he wanted to talk to you about?" Colonel Primrose asked.

"He never got to it. He —— I got the idea it was something that was hard for him to say. All he talked about was what a yellow-bellied son of heaven Carey Eaton had turned out to be, and what he thought of Stanley Woland and Mrs. Hilyard's match-making. He talked about his son too. He talked about him quite a long time. I knew him, you know. I kept thinking it was promethium he was going to talk about, or I'd have left sooner. But he never did."

All the time he was saying this he was looking across at Diane. I don't think he was conscious of it, or that he could have helped it if he had been.

"Did you see anyone as you crossed the bridge to M Street?"

"What?"

Colonel Primrose repeated.

"No."

"Did Mr. Hilyard have a hat?"

"Oh, I don't know!" He got to his feet abruptly.

"Yes, he had a hat. He handed me mine and said he got neuralgia if he didn't wear one."

He took a step across the room, pulled by something stronger than himself that wiped out all the bitterness and frustration of the years past. Diane raised her head and looked up at him, her face remote and unaware. He stood there, so controlled by heartbreaking effort that I don't think Diane knew what had almost happened.

He turned and went over to the window. "I'm sorry," he said. "I don't seem to be much help."

More to break the silence than anything, I said, "Then I don't see how Mr. Hilyard could have died at eleven thirty-five. Could his watch have stopped?"

"Not by itself," Colonel Primrose answered. "Mr. Hilyard was shot and killed. His watch was stopped and the hands moved back from whatever time it was. It was put back into his pocket and his body put in the canal. And that was done deliberately and with malice by the same person or persons who took Digges' hat out of his car on M Street and left it on the towing path— to point in one direction, and one only."

He got to his feet. What he said at first I didn't understand for some time.

"Thank God the human memory is not infallible. We'll go down and see Lamb, Digges." He started for the door and turned back. "Certain people have been informed, rather indirectly, that there is a bloody fingerprint on the band of Mr. Digges' hat," he said gravely. "That is supposed to be the reason Diane concealed it. I'm telling you that particularly, Mrs. Latham, because I'm putting the hat on the hall table here—the one nearest the door. I'd like you to go in and out as normally as you can all day. We'll take care of the rest of it. If you have callers, act as you always do. Don't take anything for granted, or jump to conclusions, and, above all, don't act on your own. Do you understand?"

"Yes, sir," I said.

"All right, then, Digges."

Diane got up, and as Bowen came from the window she took a step forward. "Bowen," she said. Her face raised to his was very pale, her eyes blue as the Caribbean. She was simple and straightforward and without dramatics of any kind.

He stopped, looking down at her. "Yes, Diane."

"Will you . . . forgive . . . all of us?"

She put out her hand, still not sure he would take it.

For a moment I thought he wasn't going to. Then he put out his. I suppose it was some such simple physical contact they both needed, for in an instant the whole room was electric. I saw his grip tighten and his body tense. Her eyes were wide, and her lips parted.

"Diane!"

It was a command and an appeal both at the same time, from the deepest part of him to the depths of her. He drew her to him, not gently but with a controlled violence of power that shattered all the barriers between them in a liberating surge that was as poignant as it was passionate. Then, with a sob, she was in his arms.

"Oh, Bowen, I love you!"

"Diane!" he said. It was all he could say, and he kept saying it again and again, as if it was all he needed, because it said everything there was.

Out in the hall, Colonel Primrose was smiling his urbane smile as he put Bowen's hat on the table.

"Do you have to take him away?" I asked.

"I'm afraid so. I wish it could have waited. He's not out of it by any means. Still, he's got something to live for now. It's hard to defend a man who doesn't give a damn."

I saw he was right when Bowen left—a new man in a brave new world. The staggering difference in him almost made up for the disturbing gravity of Colonel Primrose's face.

And Diane stood lost in a radiant fog until the door closed behind them and I came back into the room. She was so beautiful that I almost felt frightened. She closed her eyes and stood there. I suddenly realized that the tears were pouring from under her lashes in streams without her ever making a sound. "Darling!" I said.

She buried her head in my shoulder, crying, I suppose, for the first time in the whole long five years. It was Lilac who finally came and took her upstairs.

I stood looking out of the window at the bleak bare garden and the high brick wall at the end of it. I was badly worried. I don't know when anything that should have been so lovely and inspiriting had seemed so dark and ominous. I was still there when Lilac came down.

"Now she can res'. She can res' to her content," she said. "She sleepin' like a baby. . . . That ol' debbil!"

Which old devil she meant I wasn't sure. I suspected it was Colonel Primrose, but I thought it best not to inquire.

23

IF I WERE TO BE ALLOWED TO LIVE CERTAIN days of my life over again, that day would not be one of the ones I'd choose. Trying to act normally made life suddenly seem frightfully dull, and made me realize what a lot of time I wasted. Each time I went out and came back I looked at the hat, still there on the table. Lilac would come tiptoeing up from the kitchen with the phone calls and messages. Bowen had called Diane twice, but she was still asleep and Lilac wouldn't wake her. Stanley had called me once, and wanted me to call back when I came in.

Otherwise there was just the usual sort of thing. I went out to lunch, came home, went to War Relief and came home from that about four o'clock. Mrs. Hilyard had phoned to see if Diane was there. They were frantic, she told Lilac. I suppose Lilac was acting under instructions, because she said Diane was not there—which is more than I can get her to do for me. It was I who finally insisted Diane call her mother.

She'd met some old school friends, she said, and had lunched with them and was staying downtown for tea and dinner. She'd probably be home late. The new lilt to her voice must have surprised her mother into believing anything. Until she thought it over, at any rate— for ten minutes later Joan Eaton called and asked for Diane, as if she knew she was there. And Lilac lied as blandly as before.

I skipped a tea I'd been going to go to, and I was sorry I had. As the time wore on and the edge of expectancy Diane had waked with wore off, she became so quiet and still, sitting in the corner of the old sofa in the boys' room upstairs, that I found myself getting as jittery as Stanley had been in the morning. As the winter dusk settled into darkness and the street lights and lights on cars came on, she got up and knelt down on the cushion, staring out the window into the bare forlorn branches of the trees, like a lonely child waiting for someone who could never come again.

Once she said, "Grace, you don't think, do you—— I mean, nothing can happen to him, can it? Why don't they come?" But she didn't cry any more. In a way, it might have been easier.

There was a brief moment just before Lilac came up with some sandwiches and salad on a tray for us. Colonel Primrose called. We were to stay upstairs, he said. He didn't sound hopeful. We were to go to bed at the usual time. He didn't want Diane to leave the house if she hadn't left already. When I said she hadn't, he let Bowen talk to her a few minutes. That didn't last long. It seemed even to sink her deeper into silence and despair.

"If we only knew something," she whispered once. She'd given up all pretense at reading after her eyes had been glued to the same spot on the same page for half an hour.

It was exactly eight-thirty when Sheila raised her head and growled softly.

Diane's body went taut. She sprang up as if she knew what she was supposed to do, switched off the light and opened the door a few inches. The light in the upstairs hall was already off. Only the lights on the tables in the hall downstairs were on.

I could hear Lilac come up, grumbling heavily, and pad along in her felt bedroom slippers.

There was a silence as she opened the door. Then I heard her say, "No'm. She ain' home. She gone out to the movies."

I couldn't make out who it was at the door.

"Yes'm. You can wait. She won' be gone long."

I slipped off my shoes as Diane had done, crept cautiously over to the door and out to the mahogany rail at the head of the stair well. Diane was there ahead of me. I saw her raise her hand to her mouth, her other hand clutching the rail. We could see just a small part of the lower hall—only that reflected in the mirror on the paneled wall beside the door leading to the kitchen. But it reflected the opposite wall and the table that Bowen's hat was on, and just then it reflected the image of the woman who was walking past it into the living-room door. It was Mrs. Hilyard.

I caught Diane's trembling arm and shook my head, though my own face must have been as white as hers. Colonel Primrose had said we weren't to jump to conclusions. Mrs. Hilyard hadn't even glanced at the hat. She went directly on into the living room. Lilac closed the door and padded across the hall to her kitchen door.

Diane didn't move. It didn't seem to me that she was even breathing any more. Then suddenly I felt her body go as taut as a bowstring. The living-room door was opening, so slowly and silently that for an instant I could have thought it was opening by itself. Then a hand came slowly out. It grasped the white fluted wood of the frame and held it. The door still opened. My heart went very cold. Those hands! I'd noticed them the first day I called in Prospect Street—strong, purposeful, determined.

So silently that it didn't seem possible to me that a human being could move that way, Mrs. Hilyard came out into the hall. She stood there, still holding to the doorframe, listening intently. I could faintly hear the rumba coming cheerfully from Lilac's radio downstairs. Mrs. Hilyard went with quick noiseless steps to the kitchen door and bent down, listening. She came back, as quickly and as silently, to the hall table, raised her head to listen again for an instant, and seized the hat. She turned quickly, held it in the light and looked inside it. Her hands were steady as iron.

She gave one quick sideways glance at the kitchen door, folded the hat with two unhurried motions, and before I could be sure I'd really seen the unbelievable and terrifying smile of triumph on her pale face reflected in the mirror, she was gone. The front door closed as quietly as the other one had opened.

I left Diane standing there, ran back into the boys' study and pulled back one edge of the window curtain. I could see her distinctly. She was just stepping off the bottom step onto the sidewalk. She gave one glance to the left and right and walked coolly across the sidewalk to her car. And my heart sank. Colonel Primrose had slipped up, for, except for her, there was no one in the street.

Then I caught my breath. Ten yards farther down, a man stepped out of the shadows. His hat was pulled over his forehead, his overcoat collar turned up, his hands in his pockets. He took three quick steps along the sidewalk, looked quickly back over his shoulder, and then, just as my heart gave a kind of primitive, savage thrill at the idea that Mrs. Hilyard wasn't going to get away with it after all, he leaped at her with a kind of animal savagery just in the movement of his body. Mrs. Hilyard swung round, and I saw his hand rise and fall, and I screamed as she crumpled to the ground. He leaned over her, picked up the hat and stuffed it into his pocket with one swift motion, turned and ran down the street. Mrs. Hilyard lay there motionless.

It was so swift and deadly that I couldn't believe it at all, and then Diane was there, shaking me.

"What is it Grace? What is it?"

I pointed down to the street. Men were running up now, and bending over her.

"Oh, Grace, it's mother! They've killed her too!"

It wasn't Diane's mother I was thinking about; it was the man with his hat pulled down on his face and his coat collar up, creeping up in the street behind Mrs. Hilyard and striking her down, and I realized with a sudden thrill of horror that, impossible as it was, the man was Stanley Woland. And it was I myself who'd let him know the hat was at my house, and who'd warned him that Colonel Primrose knew it. That was why he hadn't come. It was all so desperately clear. And I knew now why he didn't want the bloodstains on Bowen's coat to point to him.

I went slowly across the room and slipped my shoes on. Downstairs I could hear voices already, and the tramping of feet. They were bringing Mrs. Hilyard in. I got halfway down the stairs and stopped. Colonel Primrose was coming in. Bowen Digges with him. Two men I'd never seen were carrying Mrs. Hilyard into the living room. Diane slipped past me and ran down the stairs; Bowen went quickly to meet her.

Colonel Primrose stopped at the newel post, waiting for me. His face was so grave that my heart sank deeper.

"Did he . . . get away?"

Colonel Primrose shook his head. "By no means," he said. His voice was as urbane as ever, but there was a grimness to it that I hadn't often heard. "He didn't get away, the sneaking scoundrel. He almost added a third to the list."

"Mrs. Hilyard," I said quickly. "Is she——"

"She'll live."

Outside the open door I heard the scraping of feet then, and heavy voices. A car door opened. They were crossing the sidewalk then and coming up the steps. I ran quickly down. Colonel Primrose went with me to the door. I've never seen his face so cold with anger and contempt before.

Captain Lamb was standing by the open door of the car in front. Sgt. Phineas T. Buck was coming up the sidewalk and, beside him, his hat still down, walking along with one wrist shackled to Sergeant Buck's, was Stanley. They went straight to the car. I watched them breathlessly, with a kind of cold horror. And then, as Stanley started to get in the car, he struck his head against the top of the door, and his hat was knocked off and rolled on the sidewalk. He bent down to get it, turning toward me, and in the light from my windows I saw him clearly. The strong jaw and hard mouth, the black hair shot with gray, the dark sun-tanned face.

I turned slowly to Colonel Primrose. "Bartlett Folger!"

He nodded coolly and closed the door. "The wicked was spreading himself like a green bay tree," he said.

"But, colonel!"

"But, Mrs. Latham! You told me so yourself."

24

"I DON'T THINK HE MEANT TO KILL YOU, Mrs. Hilyard," Colonel Primrose said. It was as damning faint praise as I ever hope to hear. "The doctor says you are able to answer a few questions. I'd like to get things cleared up now."

His manner was not sympathetic—as I hadn't expected it would be—and it occurred to me that he wanted to ask his questions before she had time to think things over.

And I'm happy to say that for just once I was right.

It was just after midnight. Mrs. Hilyard was propped up on my sofa. Captain Lamb had come back. Diane was sitting by her mother, and Bowen Digges was across the room, watching every move she made and every breath she took.

"I think you've been almost criminally foolish. I'm giving you a chance now to make up for it a little."

Mrs. Hilyard's thin lips tightened. She closed her eyes.

"You knew Magnussen was not a beggar, and you knew why he was here. Your brother paid him a thousand dollars, five years ago. It was that thousand dollars he had been saving to pay back since he got religion at Ira Colton's plant. That was three years ago. He told Colton there was plenty of promethium to be had. Colton thought you people were hoarding it. You weren't. I'd gone into that story, and so had about every other intelligence officer. Colton had it wrong, and Magnussen didn't explain because he was involved. When did Mr. Hilyard learn what was going on?"

"Not until a short time ago," Mrs. Hilyard said quietly.

"Which is when he decided to resign," Colonel Primrose went on. "That's why he was upset and unhappy, and thought he was responsible for the death of his own son and of other people's sons, on Sunday, December seventh, 1941. He thought that he was responsible for the scarcity of promethium—and if we'd been able to experiment with it and use it the last three years, that and other things might not have happened."

Mrs. Hilyard looked at him silently.

"He was not responsible, however. It was your brother, Folger. And yourself, Mrs. Hilyard, and the Eatons."

"We didn't know until a year ago," she said painfully. "My brother told me then. I talked to Carey. We all agreed not to tell my husband. It would ruin us. It was my money. I didn't want to lose it."

"I understand that perfectly," Colonel Primrose said. There was a shade of dryness in his voice that I'd seldom heard either.

Diane moved on the sofa. "What are you talking about?"

"We are talking about a process for extracting promethium," Colonel Primrose said deliberately, "that was pigeonholed by Bartlett Folger, who was manager of the Promethium Corporation's plant, because it would increase the available supply of promethium I don't know how many hundredfold."

Bowen Digges got slowly to his feet, staring at him.

"It would bring the price of promethium from thirty-eight dollars a pound to about seventy-five cents a pound. It was a process that a young employee worked out at your plant five years ago. His name was Bowen Digges, and that process of his was the real reason that he was paid twenty-five hundred dollars to leave town."

Bowen took a step forward. "You're wrong about that, colonel," he said, very slowly. "That process went bad. I happen to know that."

Colonel Primrose shook his head calmly. "No," he said. "It didn't. The same being the entire point of all this business. You thought it went bad. When you left your electric furnace on the last night, Magnussen was paid one thousand dollars by Bartlett Folger to turn off the heat for three hours, and turn it on then, so that you knew nothing about it. Mr. Carey Eaton was kind enough to tell me that, this evening at six o'clock—to keep himself from going to jail. . . . That is correct, Mrs. Hilyard?"

Her face was as white as the towel over the ice pack

on her head. Bowen Digges stood there, his face hard and white with anger. Diane got up slowly and moved away from her mother to the arm of my chair. She didn't say anything or look at Bowen. I took her hand, icy and inert.

"Digges was half out of his mind because he thought Diane had let him down," Colonel Primrose went on evenly. "As Mr. Folger told Mrs. Latham, he went around as if he'd been stunned. When this experiment of his went bad, it was another blow. And that's why you didn't want Diane to marry Bowen Digges. That and the fact that you were snobs."

"But we'd have been ruined!" Mrs. Hilyard cried. "We put all my money into it! You don't——"

"As a matter of fact," Colonel Primrose said politely, "in the present situation you'd have made a great deal more money. You couldn't foresee it, of course. Well your husband was the only one of you with the courage, or the patriotism, to put his country above private gain. That was the reason Folger killed him. And he wasn't content to kill one man or two. He tried to destroy a third, deliberately and wickedly. As long as Bowen Digges lived and was in a strong position in the promethium world, there was always the danger that he'd work on his old experiment again. For you hadn't patented his process. You couldn't."

Diane drew a chair up and sat down by me. All the vision and the dream of that day was gone. It had gone for Bowen too. He was tight and hard again, and the old bitterness that I hadn't recognized until it was gone had come back.

"There's your motive," said Colonel Primrose. "I'll tell you what happened. You and Mrs. Eaton left the Samarkand with Folger at twenty minutes to twelve. You got home. Mrs. Eaton stayed in the car. Your brother went inside with you. Carey Eaton was there. He told you what had happened about Diane and Stanley Woland. He stayed with you, Mrs. Hilyard, while Bartlett Folger took Mrs. Eaton home. Carey Eaton hated Digges, too, for the simple reason that he'd played a cruel trick on him. He didn't see Mr. Hilyard take the gun from Bowen. My guess is that he didn't see Folger take the gun from the desk. I don't think that Folger would have trusted him that far. He did get it, however.

"He then took Mrs. Eaton home and went down to the canal, where he knew Hilyard walked Diane's dog. He found Bowen Digges' car parked there and took his hat. That was a stroke of luck; all the rest of it was carefully prearranged. He waited until Bowen left Hilyard whistling for the dog. Then he showed. This is reconstruction, but I think it's accurate. He proposed to Hilyard that they drive along until they saw the dog on the towing path. They drove down the road, on this side of the canal, to where a boat was tied, and crossed over to find the dog. That would take only a minute. They walked along the towing path, and there, in as lonely a spot as you'll find in the district, Bartlett Folger shot his brother-in-law. He stopped the watch, set the hands back to the time Bowen had been there, and put the body in the water. He then took Hilyard's hat and left Digges', and crossed the canal again in the skiff.

"And on that skiff he left three bloody fingerprints. I'd thought they were left by the police who brought the body across the canal, until Folger made one very bad blunder when he was talking to Mrs. Latham on the Samarkand." He looked over at me with a faint smile. "He told her that Digges was on the towing path with Mr. Hilyard that night. It's about the one time his memory failed him. For the only people who knew that, were Digges, Captain Lamb, Diane, Mrs. Latham, Buck, myself, and the murderer. And none of those people had told Folger. He could only have known it by being there himself.

"Well, I think you thought it was suicide at first, Mrs. Hilyard, and you thought later it was your son-in-law. Mr. Carey Eaton thought it was you, but it didn't make much difference to him, one way or the other. He was interested always in Mr. Carey Eaton. He was quite willing to have Digges take the blame."

Diane moved painfully.

"There were several other things pointing to Folger," Colonel Primrose said. "A patrol car saw Mrs. Hilyard leave her house at two o'clock in the morning. It followed her to the Samarkand. When Mrs. Latham told me Mrs. Hilyard had been talking to Magnussen in the garden that night, it was obvious she'd gone to tell her brother. And when Folger pretended he thought the man was a beggar, I knew he was lying. He knew, of course, that the man had come to see him.

"Magnussen was a simple man. He didn't want to harm anyone, not even the people who had caused him to sin. He wanted a personal atonement. And when Folger used that word 'atonement,' talking to Mrs. Latham, it was evidence in itself. I don't suppose he'd ever used it in his life before. He will now learn what it means."

He looked at Captain Lamb.

"Will you call your men? I think the Carey Eatons are expecting Mrs. Hilyard. I should like to say also that my first interest was to check the rumor that there was promethium somewhere. My second was to keep Bowen Digges for use in his present job, and not smirched by as cowardly and malignant a conspiracy as I've run into."

Mrs. Hilyard got painfully to her feet. She looked at Diane.

"I'm sorry, mother. I can't come now. I'll come . . . later."

Mrs. Hilyard steadied herself, tried for an instant to speak, and went out with Captain Lamb.

Diane got up and went over to Colonel Primrose. "Thank you so much," she said. "Good night, Grace. And good-by, Bowen. I haven't anything to say. You must hate us all—oh, terribly."

Bowen looked at her. "Sit down, Miss Hilyard," he

said, his face slowly breaking into a grin. "With promethium down to seventy-five cents a pound, you're going to need somebody to support you."

She looked at him, her face blank and unhappy. He came over and put his arms around her.

"There, there, honey child. Come on, let's walk around the block. Mrs. Latham won't care if you get in late, and tomorrow I'm going to marry you."

"There's a fire upstairs in the boys' study," I said. "Just turn out the porch light when you leave."

"Well," I said, "that's that, then."

Colonel Primrose smiled.

"Yes. And I still haven't got around to asking you to marry me."

"Then why don't we leave it till another time?" I said.

I hadn't realized, though I should have, that Sgt. Phineas T. Buck had come back with Captain Lamb, and taken a guard duty in the hall. Or perhaps the doors and windows were all open and the thermostat set at zero. It was awfully cold, all of a sudden. And the noise like a Gargantuan jeep crossing a cast-iron bridge was Sergeant Buck clearing his throat.

"Good night, colonel," I said.

"Good night, my dear. And thanks; I couldn't get along without you."

Made in United States
Cleveland, OH
06 November 2025

25358142R00142